STREET PARTY KILLER

A chilling crime thriller with a stunning final twist

EMMY ELLIS

DI Bethany Smith Book 5

Originally published as *Death is a Party*

JOFFE BOOKS

Revised edition 2023
Joffe Books, London
www.joffebooks.com

First published in Great Britain in 2019
as *Death is a Party*

This paperback edition was first published
in Great Britain in 2023

This book is a work of fiction. Names, characters, businesses, organizations, places and events are either the product of the author's imagination or are used fictitiously. Any resemblance to actual persons, living or dead, events or locales is entirely coincidental. The spelling used is British English except where fidelity to the author's rendering of accent or dialect supersedes this.

Cover art by Dee Dee Book Covers

ISBN: 978-1-83526-159-0

PROLOGUE

Noise. It got on your nerves.
Too much. Maddening.

If those fuckers didn't go inside soon, David was likely to go mad.

His scalp itching from his headgear didn't help. Annoying but a necessity.

Under the cover of darkness, he stared through the hedge in his back garden, at them, the Party People as he'd taken to calling them. Drinking, they were, heads tilted back, same as the beer bottles and wine glasses, a seemingly never-ending stream of booze. The owner of the house had a 'do' every bloody weekend during the summer, music blaring, laughter ringing out, sometimes right into the extreme early hours. It wasn't on. Wasn't fair. Kids lived round here, nippers who needed their sleep, their parents, too.

Who worked all week to have their Saturdays and Sundays ruined by these twats?

Many a Sunday he stumbled about as though he had a hangover, and he hadn't even touched alcohol. It was the lack of a good rest that did it.

Selfish wankers. They need sorting.

That woman there, the one with the bright-red lips. Amanda her name was — he knew that from the number of times people had said it over the years. She got on his wick the most. Her laughter, it grated on him, so much so that he gritted his teeth until it hurt whenever she let it loose. It resulted in a headache, and she had no idea how her trilling, drunken giggles upset him. Ringing the police had done sod all. The bobbies came out, asked them to turn down the tunes, keep their voices low, then the moment the patrol car drove off, up it went again. Ear-splitting levels.

Murderous levels.

Something had to be done. David had been thinking about it for a long time. How to end it. End them.

That bloke, Craig, fond of golf he was, brought a microphone out, the lead trailing into the house. Everyone else cheered, a few taking up the chant: Sing, sing, sing!

Eff me, they're only going to have a sodding karaoke at two in the morning.

David clenched his fists.

Craig nodded to someone inside, and the melody of The Righteous Brothers' *Unchained Melody* blared out.

Of all the songs to pick . . .

Someone from down the way shouted, "Shut the hell up, will you? People are trying to *sleep* here!"

The gathering roared, finding it funny, and someone called out, "Piss off!"

Craig wailed out the first line.

I can't take anymore. It has to start tonight. I'm ready.

David switched his attention to all the others. They warbled along with Craig, having a right good time of it, and while David enjoyed a get-together, there were limits. You didn't naff off your neighbours. You had a bit of respect and called it a night at a reasonable hour.

He thought about his blue chair, the one he sat on to mark students' papers, also where he enjoyed peace and quiet while reading. No chance of that happening, not at the moment, with this lot being so inconsiderate.

Amanda laughed again, her blonde hair swaying, and she patted Jim's shoulder, stopped that God-awful noise barking out of her mouth, and bent over to whisper in his ear.

All her neighbours in the little close were there, so no one would know what David was going to do next.

She wandered towards the gate, and he had a feeling she'd be off over the road to her house, maybe to pick up more drinks. Amanda liked trips to France for duty-free wine. She'd have plenty to keep the gang happy for weeks to come.

David had the urge to follow her again, like he'd done before. A test run last time, but now? The real thing.

Opening his own gate to the right, he stepped into the alley. Dashing down it in reverse, he then looked up at the rear windows of the houses in his row. No one appeared to be staring out.

Good.

He turned to face the other way, and Amanda was having a bit of difficulty opening her front door. She was that pissed, she couldn't get the key in the lock. Anger burning inside him, David kept to the shadows and skirted the grass semicircle that started where he stood and ended opposite the party house, beside Amanda's drive. No streetlamp there. No one to see him unless a partygoer came along.

She'd managed to unlock the door. It bashed against the internal wall, and he winced at how she just didn't care. That could be damaged. Keith, her boyfriend, the owner of the party house, would be the one to fix it, to plaster then paint. Maybe that was why she didn't give a shit because she didn't have to worry about the mess she made. It wasn't any skin off her nose.

Bitch.

She tottered down her hallway into the kitchen at the back, the white, cheesy ball of the moon visible through the lead-paned window in there. It was smiling, the silly bastard, and David reckoned it was in encouragement: *Go on, mate, do her in. Shut her up.*

Fuelled by the moon, he ran, entering her house, using his gloved hand to close the door and then lock it. The last thing he needed was Keith coming along to investigate. Still, if he did, that'd be two less to listen to at the wretched gatherings. He could snuff *him* out an' all while he was at it. Two birds. One stone.

"Is that you?" Amanda called.

Yes, it was, but not who she thought.

She appeared in the doorway, a wine bottle held up in each hand. She swayed, her slender figure a silhouette. The dozy cow hadn't switched on a light.

Shame she wouldn't get to see what he had on his noggin.

He advanced, snatching the bottles off her, then raising one, bringing it down on the side of her head. She let out a pathetic whimper, not the scream he'd anticipated. Not so loud now, was she? Her opposite temple smacked into the doorframe, and she went down like a sack of shit, eyes closed, mouth hanging open, cheek to the floor tiles, a split in her skin. Bleeding. The red stuff dribbled down onto her neck.

Inconvenient.

Craig continued singing, the music and his voice filtering inside. He'd apparently lost that loving feeling now.

David rushed into the living room and peered out, keeping to the side behind the curtains. All seemed safe to proceed; the only house lit up was the venue of the party. This was going exactly as he'd planned it, apart from her bleeding. That was what years of thinking about something did for you. Precision. Calm under stress. And he wouldn't get stressed about the blood. He'd adapt.

The next step might be a tad tricky, but he'd give it a good go. If he managed it, he'd have no worries moving on to the next noisy prat.

Party People. They deserved everything they got. He thought about the others.

Enjoy the fun while you can.

CHAPTER ONE

Jim Ody was getting a bit worried. Amanda hadn't come back from collecting the wine, and she'd been ages. He'd sunk a beer since she'd gone, and that had to be a good hour ago. Craig had sung several more songs after the first two, and concern griped Jim's guts. He pushed himself out of the garden chair and headed over the road. Maybe Amanda had fallen asleep. She'd been sloshed, so it'd hardly be a surprise. It wouldn't be the first time either. She'd conked out under a bush once, the daft mare. Woke up with a spider on her cheek and screamed her head off.

At her front door, he grimaced, feeling guilty. The party was a bit loud, if he were honest. Good job all the neighbours in the close were there, really, but what about the people in the row behind? He'd always been uncomfortable about the noise level, but the others tended to wave off his concerns with phrases like: *Life is for living, not complaining!*

Well, someone complained every time during the summer, what with the police coming round with weak warnings. He couldn't blame the innocent neighbours for it. The poor sods probably only wanted a bit of kip. Those behind Le Huray Close were always invited, but none ever came. Why would they? The close folks were a tight-knit bunch, and any outsiders would probably feel like spare parts.

He knocked several times then rang the bell. With no response, he moved in front of the living room window to see if Amanda was sparko on the sofa. She wasn't. The moon shone in through the patio doors at the back, giving the area a ghostly glow, especially the grey laminate. Two bottles of wine stood on the fluffy white rug in the centre, and that struck him as particularly odd. Why would she put them there? Why not on the coffee table?

Back at the door, he tried the handle. No luck, so he pushed open the tight letterbox and peered inside. He hadn't had too much to drink tonight, and he wasn't really in a party mood, so his vision was sharper than it could have been had he downed his usual amount. With the moon shining in the kitchen, too, he had a clear view, but nothing seemed out of order. Perhaps she'd gone to bed.

A dark stain on the white doorframe caught his attention, and he squinted, as if that would help him see better. Why did people always do that?

What is that on there?

It was dark, he knew that much, and it might well be wet, going by the sheen, unless she was testing a patch with gloss paint to see how it looked.

He called through, loudly, and waited for a response.

Nothing.

Frowning, he legged it across the street to his place, going in via the back door. Craig sang *I Will Survive*, as did all the others, and Jim laughed to himself. Silly sods. Always up for a good laugh. Too much of a good laugh sometimes.

He grabbed his torch from the cupboard where he kept the hoover, the broom, and all that sort of shit. Over the road again, he shone the beam through the letterbox, aiming it at the blotch on the frame.

Red. Definitely wet.

Blood.

"Fuck," he said on an exhale, his heart clattering about. He placed the torch by the flowerbed, the light creating a circle on the red house bricks. On wobbly legs, he made it across the close and barged into the party garden, straight into Dee, who popped the remnants of what he guessed was a cocktail sausage in her mouth. She chewed, swallowed.

"Hold your bleedin' horses." She gave him the once-over. "Where's the fire?"

Jim glanced over her head in search of Keith but didn't spot him. Maybe he was having a wee. He couldn't hang about waiting for him. "I need you to come with me to Amanda's," he said quietly.

Dee narrowed her eyes, a bit unsteady on her feet. All that wine.

"I went over to Amanda's just now to see what was taking her so long when she went to get the wine, and . . . You'll see. And *shh*, I don't want to scare anyone yet."

"Ooh, we're going to scare them? Count me in." She let out an evil chuckle. "Are we going to hide in the bush and jump out? Remember when Craig did that once? Well funny."

"Not like that. Just . . . just come with me, all right?"

She frowned, hopefully getting the gist that this wasn't a bloody joke. "Oh. Oh. Well, then . . . What's going on?"

He took her by the wrist and guided her out of the garden and across to Amanda's. Picked up the torch, switched it back on, and then pointed the light through the letterbox. "What do you make of that?"

She bent at the waist and peeked inside. "What am I looking at?"

"The doorframe."

"Oh bollocks . . ." She straightened. "I'll . . . I'll go and get the key." Off she went, haring down the side of Amanda's, disappearing then reappearing seconds later, key in hand. They all left their spare keys in the back gardens. Out of breath and appearing not so pissed up now — a fright had a habit of sobering you — she opened the door and stepped inside. Flicked a switch.

The hallway lit up.

Dee strutted down it and stopped in front of the kitchen door. "Shit, that's not blood, is it?"

"Thought so." Jim's stomach churned. He stayed on the path. "What do we do?"

"Well, she must have hurt herself, mustn't she. I'll go and nose upstairs."

Dee vanished up there, while Jim popped the torch on the path and waited, guessing which rooms she was in by the tread on the floor. She materialised at the top of the steps, her face ashen.

"She's not here." She clambered down and stood beside him, her hands shaking. "Check the living room. I'll go in the back garden again. She might have fancied some air on her own and I didn't spot her before."

Jim did as she'd suggested, glad of something to do. It'd keep his mind away from thinking the worst. Or so he'd thought. His brain had other ideas, though, coming up with all manner of scenarios and throwing them at him, one after the other: Amanda wandering off after banging her head, lost and disorientated. Amanda falling in a ditch on the main road. A car knocking her flying.

Christ.

With no sign of her in the lounge, he picked up the wine bottles by their necks and carried them into the kitchen, one red, one white. The security light had snapped on in the garden, and Dee ferreted about in the bushes at the end, bending over, her arse jutting out. Jim absently put the bottles on the draining board and went to stand by the back door.

"Anything?" he called.

Dee shot out of the bush and barrelled up the grass. "No. Flipping Nora, this is scaring me now. Where the hell is she? Did you notice any blood in the hallway on the floor?"

Jim shook his head. "I didn't. Let's go and check."

With Dee following, Jim rushed through the kitchen, his heart giving him a bit of gyp, throbbing as hard as it was, and producing a stitch-like pain. The hallway floor was clean at first glance, then he spotted a smear, as though someone had trodden in it and scuffed it, or it had been wiped up with a tissue. So Amanda's wound had dripped, and she'd been with it enough to clean it.

"Fuck it," he said, pointing it out to Dee.

She widened her eyes then turned to go back into the kitchen. "Oh my bloody good God!"

"What?" Jim stared at her, his breathing going a bit funny. This lark was doing a number on him. He inhaled deeply, trying to steady his scattered nerves. If he didn't, he'd . . . His damn chest tightened, and his throat thickened.

"There's blood on that wine bottle." Dee gestured at them and then slapped her hands to her face.

"Excuse me?" He'd heard her, he just couldn't believe it. Blood on the bottle?

"Look!" Dee moved away so he could see.

Jim eased closer. Sure enough, the white wine had a swathe of red on it. "Jesus," he muttered. "What did she do to herself?" Rhetorical, didn't need an answer. He hurried back to the living room. Stepped closer to the rug. A penny-sized blob of blood clung to the pile. "There's some in here, too, but that was where the bottles were. I picked them up and put them in the kitchen."

Dee appeared in the doorway. "We should go and tell Keith."

Jim nodded. Amanda's boyfriend needed to know what was going on sooner rather than later, especially because it was clear Amanda was hurt. They left the house and entered the party garden. The atmosphere didn't seem so good now. The singing, the laughing, the music, it all swirled in Jim's head, and he took a second to steady himself by holding on to the back of a wooden chair. The roughness of it bit into his palm, and he idly thought about splinters being the devil to pull out. He didn't have any tweezers.

"You all right?" Dee asked, patting his back, a caring mother hen.

"No. Get that fucking karaoke turned off." He swallowed bile that had rudely come up.

"You salty shit," she grumbled and bustled into the house.

A few seconds later, Craig's voice trundled out of him with no musical accompaniment. A series of groans floated around, and Dee took the mic off Craig, who snapped his gob shut and stared at her, uncomprehending as to why his music was gone.

"Is everyone out here?" Dee asked, giving those gathered a quick glance.

Jim was too freaked out to do the same. He leant over, hands on his knees, staring at the grass, hoping the beers didn't join the bile and fill his mouth.

"Where's Keith?" Dee asked.

"He went up for a nap, the lightweight," someone said.

Jim stood upright and fixed his attention on Dee.

"Okay . . . Now listen." She planted her hands on her hips. "Jim went over to find Amanda . . ."

She told them the rest, and the raucous chattering died down until the only voice was hers.

"You what?" Craig said, swaying. "Blood?"

Dee nodded. "Someone go and get Keith out of bed."

Everyone seemed to move too slowly, so Jim took the lead and stormed into the house, mumbling swear words at how his friends had gone all dumbstruck, annoyed they just sat there, gawping, their brains too addled by alcohol for them to think straight. This was bloody serious, he sensed it keenly, and there wasn't time for dicking about. He pelted up the stairs, going straight for the main bedroom door. Turning the handle, he stopped without releasing the latch. If the sounds coming from inside were any indication, Keith wasn't asleep. A woman moaned, and Jim's blood ran cold. His chest tightened again, and he scrambled to make sense of the noise. It couldn't be. Just couldn't.

With a burst of courage, he flung the door open, greeted with the sight of Keith's hairy backside bobbing and a pair of legs he'd know anywhere draped around his middle. Shocking pink polish on her toenails. A mole on the ankle.

"What the fuck?" Jim couldn't breathe. Couldn't *think*.

A shriek, an "Oh shit!", and Keith jumped off Jim's bird, Melinda.

"You absolute bastard!" Jim launched himself at Keith and punched him, Keith's nose crunching beneath meaty knuckles.

Keith fell off the bed, landing on his back, and Melinda scrabbled off, too, a hand up to her mouth.

"I'm so sorry, Jim," she said. "I didn't mean to."

"Piss off, you," he said. "Of course you *meant* to. Keith, while you were shagging my missus, your *girlfriend* went missing. You might want to help find her. Or maybe not, seeing as some slapper has your attention now." Jim gave Melinda a scathing glance and then left, tromping downstairs and back out into the garden, anger forging a violent path inside him. "Keith and Melinda were busy shagging." There was no point skirting around it. He had no intention of staying with Melinda now, so there'd be no covering up. He stared at all the faces to see if any of them knew this had been going on.

All appeared shocked, but that didn't mean anything.

"Melinda and Keith?" Dee said, shaking her head.

"Fuck those two," Jim said. "I suggest we fan out in the close and look for Amanda. She's the most important one at the moment, not them."

The mood sombre, Jim led the way out of the garden, his heart heavy. He should have guessed about Keith and Melinda. They were always flirting. Jim hadn't thought much of it, though, putting it down to them looking but not touching. Well, that hadn't been the case, but he couldn't let that consume him at the minute. Like he'd said, Amanda was the important one now.

His band of neighbours headed in all directions, some going into their houses in case Amanda had wandered in there, others checking the front and back gardens. Another couple disappeared down the alley, probably to the street behind.

Jim aimed for the grass semicircle with Dee. She squeezed his shoulder, and he was grateful for her concern. She'd always been a good mate, although she had warned him Melinda seemed a bit of a flighty piece. He'd ignored her. God, he wished he'd listened now. He waited for her to say 'I told you so', but it never came. He didn't know why he'd thought she'd say that. She wasn't one for pouring salt on wounds.

"I had no idea," she said. "I'm so sorry."

"Yeah, well, shit happens."

At the back of the semicircle stood a privet hedge that blocked off the main road. It appeared to have been disturbed, as though someone had pushed through it.

"See that?" he asked. "I'll go and get my torch."

He ran to Amanda's, collected it, and jogged back. He lit up the hedge. Yep, someone had clambered through it all right. There was a wide parting, and a lot of the branches had snapped, leaving a clear enough pathway to get to the other side. A car swished along the main road, and Jim squeezed through, catching sight of the red taillights as the vehicle skirted the corner, heading for the roundabout that led to the estate. He waved his torch about, illuminating patches of the verge.

"Oh God . . ." Dee said. "Point it back that way, to the left."

Jim did, his poor heart not only broken by Melinda but protesting against the drama of this situation. The glowing shaft landed on a bare foot. He shifted it along, up a leg — a leg covered in Amanda's pink jeans. The long, scrubby grass in front of the hedge covered the rest of her.

"Fuck, fuck, fuck . . ." Jim staggered backwards. "Ring . . . ring someone." He couldn't get 'police' out, his tongue refusing to form the word. *Ambulance. Ring for one of those, too.*

Dee dashed forward, and Jim managed to follow, albeit unsteadily, and it wasn't from the drink. He was scared.

"Don't touch anything," he said. "It might be . . ."

Dee whipped her phone out, dialled, and jammed it to her ear. "Police and ambulance." A pause. "Our friend . . .

She's out on the verge bordering the Warburg estate. The main road, yes. Before the curve in the road where there's a roundabout." She took several breaths. "I don't know. She's in the grass, only her leg sticking out. We went to her house, and there was blood . . . Okay . . . Right." She looked at Jim. "I'm handing the phone to my other friend."

She shoved it at Jim, and he took it, fumbling, as though the damn thing was too hot, too heavy.

He raised it to his ear. "Hello?"

"I'll give you instructions," the woman on the other end said.

Jim steeled himself and trailed Dee, who walked forward a few metres and parted the grass. He stayed back a bit. He didn't want to see . . . What? *Amanda's dead body.*

"What can you see, sir?" the woman asked.

"Nothing. I'm not close enough."

"She's dead," Dee said.

"Dead," Jim repeated.

"The person is deceased, sir? Ask your friend to check for a pulse."

"Pulse, Dee," he managed.

"There's no point, but I'll do it anyway."

No point?

Poor Dee. She stared at him for a second, then seemed to gather her nerves and stepped forward. She knelt beside Amanda, the grass obscuring Dee's top half. Jim felt awful, but he couldn't seem to function for the life of him. Every part of him was blank.

Dee shook her head. "I can't feel one."

"There isn't one," Jim told the woman.

"Check her mouth, her airway," the dispatcher advised.

Jim repeated the instruction.

"It's clear," Dee said.

Jim related that info. "What now?"

"Do either of you know how to do CPR?" he was asked.

"Not me," he said and felt bad again.

Dee would have to be the one to do it.

With the dispatcher guiding the way, Jim passed on her messages, and Dee got to work, mumbling about it being a waste of time. It didn't take long for an ambulance to turn up, and paramedics jumped out, taking over. Dee looked relieved to have that burden lifted from her, and she cuddled into Jim's side, turning her face into his T-shirt, crying softly.

Her hands and mouth were covered in blood.

Oh God . . .

"You're a braver person than I am," he whispered. "I'm sorry, I just couldn't . . ."

"I know," Dee said. "It's okay."

They stood there like that for what seemed an age, Jim mesmerised by the ambulance's flashing lights, rubbing Dee's back as though cementing it in his head that *she* was alive, safe.

"What do you think happened?" Dee asked. "Did she see what Keith and Melinda were doing and . . . and killed herself?"

"I don't think so. She told me she was going to get more wine. She was happy, laughing. Didn't seem like an act."

"So what then? What the fuck's going on?"

"I don't know," he said. "Maybe she was so drunk she came this way and got knocked over, but that doesn't explain the blood at her house."

Dee shook her head, her cheek warm on Jim's chest. She stared up at him. "She can't have got knocked over. Not with a slit throat."

CHAPTER TWO

Bethany gritted her teeth. Who wanted to be called out in the early hours of a Sunday morning? She bloody didn't, but that was what she'd have to do — go out there and see a body on a grass verge. Ursula on the front desk had called her, saying it didn't look like a road traffic accident because the woman's throat had been cut. Isabelle, the lead SOCO, was already there, and that would mean a tent should have been erected by now. The corpse was by a main road. All right, people didn't tend to use it much at this hour, but someone might have seen something, though if they had, why hadn't it been reported? The dispatcher Ursula had spoken to had said they saw a leg poking out of the grass. It wasn't every day you saw that, was it?

From what Ursula had said, the woman had been at a party, which was a regular occurrence throughout the summer, with all the residents of the small street, Le Huray Close, attending without fail. There were numerous complaints logged about the noise and length of the parties, and other than uniforms going out to give warnings, nothing had been done.

"You'd think they'd call the sodding council instead," she muttered to herself, making a coffee for her and Mike in her Home Bargains to-go cups. She bloody loved that shop. Last week she'd got a nifty set of pegs that had a free bag. They'd come in handy. It was another hot summer. She'd get her washing dried in no time once she put the rotary line up.

She left the house and went to Mike's, sipping her drink on the way. He stood at the end of his path and got in, taking his coffee out of the cup holder automatically. She always made him a drink. It gave them some oomph before they got to a scene. A sense of normality before the shit hit the fan and the vulgar evidence of humanity's fallen blasted their senses.

While she drove, she told him what was going on.

"Throat slit?" he said. "Nice."

"Probably not nice, but I get what you're saying." She smiled. "So there will be a fair few neighbours to talk to, although apparently there are only eight houses, all of them without kids living there. We'll have to establish who has partners and whatever. Still, a lot to do, and all of them were drunk so all will have alcohol in their systems. Might not be able to trust their initial statements."

"Let's hope the two who found the body are coherent. Bloody hell, what a prospect, interviewing pissheads." He sipped. "You always make a damn good coffee."

"Remember that woman we talked to who mentioned Jersey milk? I started using it." She'd forgotten about it until recently but was glad she'd taken a gamble. She wouldn't be buying anything else now. "Anyway, talking about milk isn't going to get our heads around what's happened. Anything you want to discuss before we get there?"

He nodded. "Why did the female neighbour do CPR if the victim's throat was slit? Why didn't she say it was?"

"Panic? Was doing as she was told? Who knows? The poor woman was probably in shock. You just follow instructions in those circumstances, don't you. Authority carries weight. Anyway, we'll ask her."

"And the man who was with her. Why didn't he tell the dispatcher she was dead?"

"Again, no clue. I'm concerned that no one driving on the main road saw her leg from the light of their headlamps, if anyone even went by, but someone was there — whoever killed her."

"Hmm. They were talking a risk, parking up while dumping her, assuming that's what happened." Mike shivered.

"Someone walk over your grave?" She gulped down the remainder of her coffee.

"Probably. It's creepy out at night on a main road — limited lights. I was just thinking of the woman being there, possibly followed. The fear she must have felt . . ."

"What gets me is why she was even *on* the main road. She'd been at the party and had left to get more booze. Gone an hour before anyone noticed."

"Does she have a husband?"

"Not sure. Ah, here we are." Bethany peered ahead. A tent was indeed up, and a SOCO van parked close to the verge a few metres past it. She drew up behind it, cutting the engine.

With them both out on the road, they put on protective clothing and then walked to the tent. Nicola Eccles, a uniform, stood there with the scene log. Bethany signed it.

"Who's with the neighbours?" she asked Nicola.

"Glen. They're all at the house where the party was. The victim's has blood in it."

Mike signed in. "Where?"

"On the kitchen doorframe and a rug in the living room. Also on wine bottles." Nicola shrugged. "Maybe she used it as a weapon to fend someone off?"

"Possibly." Bethany nodded. "Could be someone at the party. Think about it, all of them drunk — you can't keep an eye on everyone. Anybody could slip off and do the deed." She sighed. "I bloody hate humans sometimes."

She held a hand up at Nicola to say bye for now and walked to the tent. Mike stood beside her and let out a ragged breath.

"Come on then," he said. "Let's see what we have here."

Bethany stepped inside first. A couple of SOCOs knelt in the grass either side of the body. Isabelle stood next to it, turned to see who'd come in and lowered her face mask using her wrist.

"Good morning to you," Isabelle said. Either she'd had an espresso to make her chirpy or she didn't mind being up at this ridiculous hour. Four-thirty on a Sunday morning should be illegal. "Although there's nothing good about this. The poor cow has two mouths. Second smiles are always bad."

Bethany stood beside Isabelle. The woman, Amanda DeBord, if Bethany remembered rightly from when Ursula had rung, rested on her back, one leg straight, the other bent, her foot tucked beneath her knee. "Morning. Is that the position she was found in?"

"Blimey, you're keen, asking questions right off the bat. No. I've been told the lady who gave CPR, a Dee Groocock, pushed her on her back to do it. DeBord was originally on her left side. As you can see, she has a wound on her right temple and a gash on the other side farther back, so she's taken a double hit."

"Could have slipped over while drunk," Mike suggested.

"Could have, which is why there's blood at her house," Bethany said. "But she didn't get that neck slice falling arse over tit."

"No," Isabelle said. "And going from experience, I'd say she didn't cut her own throat either. I'm sure Presley will take great pleasure in informing us of the same. Elvis does like to gloat, and he's going to be dogged off at being called out so early."

"Stop it with the Elvis. You know he hates it." Bethany couldn't stop a grin. "And we've all been called in, so I don't understand why he takes it out on you." She frowned.

"Because he shoots the messenger, God love him. Anyway, best not carry on talking about him. He'll be here in a bit."

Bethany gave the body her full attention. There had been no hacking, and as far as Bethany could tell, only one slice had been applied to the neck — no sign of someone sawing to get through skin, muscle, and bone. This had to be one of the most disturbing things a civilian could see, and she suspected Groocock would be suffering from trauma. Nightmares in her future, too. Perhaps even daymares.

Other than the obvious injuries, DeBord appeared unharmed. Her clothing, though bloodstained, wasn't ripped or dirty. Jeans, a cerise vest top with small twigs attached to it.

"Back in a sec." Bethany dipped out of the tent to have a look around. A hedge had a gap in it, and she walked closer, stepping around a SOCO on his knees searching through the long grass. The twigs on DeBord's top could have come from there, which was interesting. Had she walked through alone and encountered a killer? Or had she been brought through? If blood was in her house, Bethany was inclined to go with the latter, but she wouldn't put all her eggs in one theory basket. DeBord could have banged her head and wandered this way, disorientated. Just her luck someone was waiting for her, ready to kill her.

That was too convenient.

She returned to the tent.

"I was just telling Mike," Isabelle said, "that it seems like the weapon was wiped on this grass. See that?" She pointed.

Bethany peered that way. The yellowed grass, more like hay, had a faint red stripe down the middle, about two inches in depth. "Less chance of drips giving away which direction they went afterwards while carrying the blade."

Mike nodded. "I thought the same thing. There might not have been enough to drip, though. The amount on that grass is minimal. If the cut was quick . . ."

Bethany wished the image of this woman being killed would sod off out of her head. Mike had mentioned the fear earlier, and knowing you were going to be murdered was right up there with the most terrifying experiences on offer in life. Hopefully, DeBord wouldn't have suffered with pain — or not for long anyway.

The sound of a car engine plundered the tent, and she poked her head out. Presley parked down the road a bit, and she faced the interior again, staring at the back of the tent instead of DeBord.

"Presley's here," she said.

"Hope he isn't snarky." Isabelle moved back, the grass rustling against her suit. "I might just have to pull his leg if he is, wind him up some more."

"Pack it in, you," Bethany said, smiling. "It gets really uncomfortable when you two bicker."

"Ah, he needs to lighten up." Isabelle sniffed. "All that death around him every day makes him as dead in the humour department as them when he's not in the mood for a bit of a giggle."

"What was it you said earlier about being quiet in case he heard you?" Mike asked, eyebrows raised.

"I forgot about that," Isabelle said. "I'll not say another word until he comes in. What's he doing, anyway, making the damn protective suit before he puts the bugger on?"

Bethany stifled a laugh, and a SOCO coughed. No one said a thing, probably so they didn't get caught yakking about the ME. Isabelle got a fit of the sillies, her shoulders bobbing, and she put her mask back in place — to hide her ruddy great smile, no doubt.

"Stop it!" Bethany whispered. What was it with certain situations where when you shouldn't laugh, you wanted to?

The man himself strode in, teeth on show, eyes bright.

Fugging hell. What's got him so chipper?

"Morning," he trilled.

"Um, morning . . ." Isabelle lowered her eyebrows, clearly confused at his demeanour. "Get your leg over last night, did you?"

"That's a bit personal for a Sunday," he said. "A bit personal any day. Why do you ask?"

"Because you're happy," Isabelle said. "When I call you out early, you're never like this."

"Well, today I am." He took his clipboard out and got on with sketching the body. "Or maybe I'm pretending to be happy so you don't get on my back. You'll never know." He winked, shoved his face mask up, and hummed.

"Well, I'll be . . ." Isabelle said.

"What size knife would you say was used?" Mike asked, probably to stop Isabelle saying anything more. "It's just that the length of the stripe smeared on the swathe of grass is a bit long."

"Might be a sword, something like that," Presley replied. "Pretty sharp to go through the spine. Nasty. Still, she'd have barely registered the pain. It would have all been over in a few seconds."

"She was intoxicated," Bethany said. "That could have dulled her senses."

"I thought I could smell wine." Presley glanced at Isabelle. "Suspected you'd had a skinful before coming out. I know how much you like the white stuff."

"Cheeky sod," Isabelle huffed. "I'll have you know, I didn't have anything but coffee last night, and I went to bed early. Must have had a premonition about getting a work call. Is that what you did, too? Seems to me you've had plenty of sleep to be this amenable."

"Like I said, you'll never know." Presley put his clipboard away. "Am I okay to move her?"

Isabelle nodded. "We're done with her immediate area."

While Presley took DeBord's temperature, Bethany said to Mike, "We're going to have to get going soon. People to talk to."

He nodded.

"Death between two and three," Presley said. "She's either banged her head herself or has been pushed into something that split the temple skin. Look at that there — a couple of lines."

"There's blood on her doorframe," Mike said.

"That rings true for these marks." Presley leant forward. "On the other side is a contusion and split scalp indicating a wallop, obviously with something hard and heavy."

Bethany thought about what Nicola had said. "A wine bottle?"

"Could be." Presley pushed DeBord onto her right side. "I'd bet her neck was sliced while she was prone. Plenty of blood soaked into the grass beneath her head, although it isn't consistent either side. It's more prevalent here" — he pointed — "and while there's some on the right, it's indicative of the slice, then a quick shove so she's on her left."

"That marries with what we've been told," Isabelle said. "Are *you* getting married, Pres? That'd make anyone cheerful."

"Be quiet, Isabelle," he said. "Prodding for me to slip up isn't going to work."

"Balls to you." She lowered her mask again and stuck her tongue out.

"Okay, time we were leaving." Bethany waved and left the tent.

They signed out of the log, and at the hedge, she asked the SOCO, "All right to go through here now?"

"Yeah. It's been checked and cleared."

"Thanks." She squeezed through, glancing over her shoulder at Mike. "Tight fit."

"That was an eighties band."

"What?" She waited for him on the other side.

"Tight Fit. A pop group. You know, *The Lion Sleeps Tonight*."

"Oh, for fuck's sake, behave, will you? I've got a sodding earworm now."

"A whim-a-way, a-whim-away . . ."

"Shut it, Wilkins." She jabbed him in the ribs. "Lucky for us, the next of kin is abroad on holiday. Ursula checked for me. I didn't fancy visiting them just now."

"Me neither."

She surveyed the area.

A half circle of grass led to the road, and four houses were on either side, pretty large, giving the place an affluent feel. An alley on the left went down past the closest house, and lights shone from every window. Directly opposite, another house was lit up, but the rest sat in darkness. Tory Yates stood outside the right-hand one, so Bethany headed there.

"I take it that's the victim's pad," she said.

Mike walked next to her. "Hmm. Glen's at the party house. Probably inside."

"Morning, Tory." Bethany signed the log. "Many SOCOs inside?"

"Three," Tory said, passing the log to Mike. "How is it out there?" She jerked her head at the hedge.

"You don't really want to know, do you?" Mike asked.

"Probably not." Tory grimaced.

Bethany grabbed a fresh pair of booties by the door, seeing as there were two scenes. She didn't want a bollocking for contaminating this one. She dropped her others in the paper bag provided then stepped inside. An evidence marker squatted by what appeared to be a scuff of blood. She lifted her head and took note of the scarlet matter on the kitchen doorframe. That must have hurt, bumping her head on there. Temples were sensitive buggers. Skirting past the floor scuff, she entered the kitchen, where a SOCO dusted the back door for prints. The two wine bottles were on the draining board, one with a flash of red at the base. Seemed like short white hairs had latched on to the fluid.

She turned, expecting to see Mike, but he wasn't there. She called out to him.

"In here," he said.

Bethany walked to the living room. Mike stood beside a rug, staring down.

"Look at the pattern on here," he said.

Bethany smiled at the SOCO in the corner then gazed down. Two circles had flattened the rug pile, and a spot of blood, plus a thin curve of it, wrecked the pristine whiteness.

"The wine bottle bases," she said. "Which is why I thought hairs were on the blood. It's carpet fibres."

"Why would they be on the floor in the first place?" Mike's forehead crinkled.

"Beats me. Suppose we'd better find out. Odd place to put them."

"Life is odd," he said.

She sighed. "So is death."

CHAPTER THREE

David stood by the hedge in his garden and peered through. It was daring doing this, being out here, but he couldn't help himself.

With all the lights on in the party house, he had a good view of what was going on. The kitchen faced the back and went on into a living room on the other side of open double doors. Everyone had gathered there, some on the sofa and chairs, others standing. Another on foot was a copper, and it didn't take a genius to work out either Amanda had been reported missing or her body had been found. A ceiling fan rotated, ruffling Keith's long, scruffy hair. The stupid prat looked bored.

David's sabre, washed in bleach water in the bath, hid behind his couch. He'd dumped Amanda in the grass on the verge, then hurried home to collect his weapon. Using it for the first time on human flesh was so much better than lopping cooked chicken legs off with it or whacking into a joint of fillet beef to create steaks. The amount of blood had been gross.

He wondered whether the police would come to his street. They should, really, to check if anyone had seen anything from the rear windows. He had his story straight, and with no lamps on in his place all night, he should be believed.

Dressed in black like this, with his scuba helmet on, he doubted any of his neighbours would have seen him down here. Too dark on this side of the hedge. With the music switched off and Party People's chatter all gone, most folks would have slipped into sleep. David had done them a favour, and they'd be thankful.

The copper walked out of the living room, then came back, two others in tow. A man and a woman. They stood in front of the window in white, the red curtains a backdrop, and he fancied they were on a stage, with the Party People the audience. The woman spoke, and he lipread, something he'd learnt to do while teaching, catching the little buggers in class when they whispered at the back. He was too far away to work out everything she said, but he recognised 'bad news'.

Ah. So they'd found her. Amanda the cackler.

David turned, crouched, and soldier-crawled up his sloping garden so those in the party house wouldn't see him. He made it to the side of his, out of view, and stepped in. For the first time so far this summer, and the first summer weekend night in years, he wouldn't have to listen to that lot being noisy until daybreak. By next Saturday, none of them would be alive.

No more parties.

Lovely.

* * *

"They're just damn inconsiderate," Elaine Wilson said.

David nodded. "I couldn't agree more."

They stood in their street, putting the world to rights, like they always did post-party. The sun was being a right pig today, belting out the heat. Elaine's arms were going red, and her shoulders, well, they had to be sore.

"And you having to get up on a Monday, knackered, to teach all those kids." She folded her arms under her boobs. "It won't be long and

there'll be the school break. End of July, isn't it? You can rest during the week then." She continued before he could reply. "It shouldn't be allowed, all this party lark. I tell you, I have to nap on a Monday and Tuesday in the summer to catch up on my sleep. Must be worse for you, having them directly behind. Even me being three doors down is bad enough."

Was she bragging? Rubbing it in that he fared worse?

David shrugged that thought off. Elaine was too nice to do something like that, and he'd been cruel to think it, but that was what no sleep did for you. Got you paranoid, imagining things. Planning the deaths of those in Le Huray Close. He'd been entertaining it since year three.

"I'm telling you," Elaine went on, "I'm on the verge of filming them or at least getting a sound recording of how loud they are. I'm tempted to ring the environmental health department an' all."

David had considered doing the same thing, but he'd much rather kill them. Now the seed had been planted, it was all he thought about in his downtime. Ways to kill. How to get away with it. Come winter, all those wicked things left his head, but summer soon rolled around again, and here they were, six years into this mess with no resolution.

"Someone else rang the council last year," he said. "Nothing was done. It wouldn't be so bad if that lot seemed remorseful, but they find it funny when anyone shouts for them to shut up."

"That'll be the booze. Everyone's mouthy when they've had a few." Elaine scuffed at a loose stone on the pavement, the material flower on her pink flip-flops wobbling. "D'you know, I saw that Lisa in Sainsbury's the other day. What's her bloody surname again?"

"Hicks." David knew them all. He'd done his research. Earwigging was a valuable pastime.

"Well now, she smiled, all nice. You wouldn't think she'd told me to fuck off last weekend, would you? Did you hear that malarky?"

"I did."

"I stomped down the alley and hammered on the fence — bent over, too, and stared through a knothole, told them to turn the racket down. That Lisa, she lifted her glass of wine and said what she said, and I couldn't believe it. She's usually so quiet at keep fit."

That was news to David. How had he missed it? "She does keep fit?"

"Yes, at the community centre on a Monday night. She's in my group; that's how I know her. I was shocked by her behaviour, as you can imagine."

"Maybe someone will teach her a lesson one day."

"Like what?"

"Oh, I don't know. Just something you say, isn't it."

"I s'pose." Elaine glanced at her arms. "Oh heck, I'm bloody cooking here. Didn't put any sun cream on, did I. Was only meant to put rubbish in the bin. Didn't intend to gas for so long. I'd best be off. A cold bottle of raspberry lemonade has my name on it. Blimey, when will this weather let up, eh?"

She waved and walked up her path, leaving the rubbish bag by her gate.

"Oh, ruddy hell!" She turned and trounced back. "I'd forget my head if it wasn't screwed on." Refuse firmly in the wheelie bin, she disappeared inside her house.

David strolled up the road a bit, waiting for someone to spot him so he could talk about Party People some more. Sadly, after five minutes of him loitering, he gave in and went home. Maybe everyone was having a kip. Last night's party had been particularly loud, lasting until seven this morning. That Lisa bloody Hicks had gone inside and brought out a plate full of toast, a tray of tea, and David had seethed at how normal it had all appeared, neighbours meeting for breakfast. Except they were drunk and using the food to soak up the alcohol.

He had some marking that needed doing so set up his small folding table in front of his blue chair. Whether he'd be able to concentrate remained to be seen. Still, there wasn't much to do, and if he could keep his mind on that for the next hour, he could think about killing those bastards for the rest of the day.

Later, his eyes gritty and heavy, he packed away the papers and his red pen. Made a strong coffee, then retook his seat. It faced the patio doors, and as his house was on a rise, he had the perfect view into the party venue.

Someone was in the kitchen there, at the sink, he reckoned. What were the odds, eh? It was Miss Lisa Hicks, acting right at home. You'd think she'd make herself scarce, give Keith and his missus a bit of time to themselves. Mind you, Lisa was single, and Keith had a roving eye, so maybe he encouraged her to hang around with them. He'd copped a feel of Lisa's bum last night about ten o'clock. His bird had been too busy scoffing triangle-shaped sandwiches to notice, but Craig had clocked it, nudging Dee, who'd shook her head, clearly disgusted.

Shame she wasn't disgusted enough to care about the noise level. None of them were, although, to be fair, that Jim fella, he wasn't one of the worst offenders. That didn't matter, though. He was on the list just for attending the parties, week in, week out.

Year in, year out.

David closed his eyes and thought of all the ways he'd end them.

A smile stretched wide, and he drifted off to sleep with his head on the back of the chair, hoping to dream about his scenarios in glorious technicolour.

* * *

"What do you think about mass murder?" David asked his colleague, Alan Hughes, science teacher and all-round good bloke.

Alan looked up sharply from his tablet and placed it on the staffroom table. "Er, beg your pardon?"

David almost laughed at Alan's horror-stricken expression. He'd have to play this carefully to throw Alan off the real reason he was asking. "You know, when people go into public places and kill. We're teachers. We should be worried. America could be right on our doorstep in a few years if we don't watch ourselves."

Alan visibly relaxed. "True. It's something we need to think about more. Mind you, we've been having drills for that sort of thing, so—"

"What sort of person does it, do you think?"

"They've got a screw loose, that's what I think." Alan frowned. "They have to in order to plan it, act it out."

David didn't have a screw loose, and he'd planned it. He was yet to act it out, but he still wasn't mad, just angry, pissed off with being kept awake. "Don't you wonder whether the shooters have just had enough and feel the need to do it?"

"I can't say I've thought about it much." Alan picked up his tablet, a signal for David to shut up. He always did that when he didn't want to talk.

But David wanted to talk. "Why not? It could affect you. Someone could walk into this school after lunch and blow everyone to pieces with an assault rifle."

"And that's why I don't think about it." Alan huffed. "The thought of any of our students — or us teachers — getting blown to pieces isn't something I want to consider. I care about everyone here, so to deliberately imagine that . . ."

"Would you feel sorry for the shooter?"

Alan dropped the tablet a little too forcefully. "I doubt it."

"Not even if they had a valid reason?"

"What the hell valid reason could they have to kill people like that?"

David smiled. "Blimey, don't get all lairy. I just wanted to have a civilised conversation about something that is important to me."

"Then I'm not the person you need to speak to."

Alan got up, put his tablet into his satchel, and stalked out of the room.

David would have to be careful. Alan was against the sort of thing David wanted to do. In future, he'd pretend he found it abhorrent as well. He'd slipped up in his excitement, in his obsession with his plan. It wouldn't do for Alan to suspect David down the line after he'd killed the Le Huray bunch.

He didn't chastise himself too much, though. This was all new to him, a learning curve. He was bound to make a few rookie mistakes.

CHAPTER FOUR

"We'll speak to you one at a time, briefly, then get full statements after you've all had some sleep," Bethany said. "Who would like to go first?"

She'd already told them there was bad news but hadn't explained what it was. Best to get their initial reactions one-on-one — and see who was willing to talk without being approached to do so.

A man stood from the sofa, his hair long, dark, and tangled, a nasty black eye forming. His nose leant slightly off centre.

"Me," he said.

"And your name is?" Bethany raised her eyebrows.

"Keith Trannor. I'm Amanda's boyfriend."

Oh. Closer to home for him then. "Is there somewhere we can go for privacy?"

"The kitchen?" He pointed at a set of double doors.

Bethany looked that way. Everyone's reflection appeared ghostly in the kitchen window beyond. It was one of those things she'd recall later, perhaps, a pivotal moment amongst so many people whose lives were going to be affected by what she had to tell them.

She nodded and picked her way through those present, knowing Mike would gesture for Keith to follow. Once in the room, she closed one of the doors and waited for the men to file in, then shut the other. Keith leant against the sink unit under the window, while Mike stood by the fridge freezer. With the absence of a table and chairs, she could only hope Keith didn't lose his shit from the shock and slump to the floor.

"What time did you notice Amanda had left the party?" she asked.

He coloured up at that. Cleared his throat. "Err, I didn't."

"Why not?"

He rubbed his nose. "I was in bed."

"I see. Do you usually leave your own party like that?"

He shrugged. "Sometimes. We're all mates. Known each other for yonks. I don't mind them carrying on when I'm not there."

"How long have you been seeing Amanda?"

"About three years. She lives opposite."

We know. "How is your relationship?"

"So-so."

"Please explain that to us." This didn't sound too good. If their relationship wasn't stellar, could he have killed her? Lied about being in bed? Bumped her off while everyone else was distracted by booze and good company?

"On the wane, to be honest." He sighed, his expression tightening with . . . guilt?

"Why?"

"Growing apart, I s'pose." He rammed a hand into his hair, and it got stuck in the knots. He must have tossed and turned in that bed of his for it to be in such a state.

"Was Amanda aware of that?"

Had the poor woman picked up on the signs that her boyfriend didn't feel the same about her? Was that why she'd gone to get wine, to drown her sorrows even more?

"No idea." Keith sucked in his bottom lip and had a good old gnaw on it.

"Were you intending to split up with her?"

"Yeah. I'm seeing someone else. It's got a bit serious. We can't keep sneaking around the way we have."

She hadn't expected *that.* "Who is it?"

"What do *you* need to know for?" He scowled.

Belligerent twat. "Please answer the question."

"Melinda Nash."

"And she is?"

"Jim's girlfriend."

"And *he* is?" Bloody hell, this was like pulling teeth. Painful.

"One of the neighbours in the close."

"Right." She remembered now. Jim Ody had been with Dee Groocock when the body had been found. There were so many people, she'd have to keep them all straight in her head or risk fucking up somewhere down the line. "Is anyone else here aware of this . . . thing you have going with Melinda?"

"Everyone. Jim came up and caught us."

"When?"

"Tonight, after he'd been to Amanda's with Dee."

What a mess. "Where did you get your black eye?"

"A present from Jim."

Good. You deserve it, you cheating bastard. "Has your nose always been that . . . skewed?"

"Nope. Probably broken."

"Probably." *That's the least of your worries.* "What I have to say next needs to be kept to yourself until everyone has been informed, including family members. Go upstairs afterwards, keep out of the way." All sympathy for him had dried up. "It's important that you do as I've said." She wasn't going to explain why. Too many others to talk to. "I'm sorry to tell you that Amanda's body was discovered on the grass verge by the main road."

He stared at her, skin whitening, and grabbed a strand of his hair, twirling it around his finger. It needed a damn good wash. Funny the things you thought about while at work.

"What?" he said, the word a croak.

"She's deceased."

"Oh fuck . . ." He pushed off the sink unit and paced, the width of the kitchen allowing four steps one way, then he had to turn. "It wasn't me."

"I didn't say it was." Was that all he cared about? Getting the blame? What a selfish individual. "As you said, you were having sex with Melinda. I'm sure she'll back that up, seeing as how you're so serious about each other."

"She will. We're in love."

"Handy, that." She sucked in a big breath. Couldn't stand to speak to him any longer. "That's it for now. Please don't even think about messaging your friends in the other room, or anyone else for that matter. Not until we're done here."

He left, slamming both doors.

"What a tosser," Mike said quietly.

"Yep. Plenty of them about, matey. Which delightful person shall we pick next?"

"Get Melinda out of the way, send her home after, then we'll speak to Ody and Groocock. We should have started with them first really."

"I agree. Let's blame it on us still being a bit tired." She smiled and opened one of the doors. "Melinda Nash?" she called out.

The woman came in, feet bare, short-shorts showing half her arse. One side of her black top had slipped, revealing a tanned shoulder, or maybe it was meant to be like that. Bethany wouldn't know. Fashion wasn't her top priority. Melinda's blonde hair was also tousled, giving credence to Keith's statement of what they'd been up to.

Bethany dug right in. "What were you doing tonight when Amanda went missing? And please don't lie."

"I was . . ." She gave a smug expression. "I was with Keith."

"Where?"

"In his bedroom."

"Doing what?" Bethany tapped her foot.

"Having sex."

"Lovely of you to do that to a friend. How do you feel about Amanda?"

"I like her."

"Yet you're happy to mess about with her boyfriend?"

"It isn't like that," Melinda snapped.

"No, it never is. When did you know Amanda hadn't come back with the wine?"

"When Jim caught us. We were doing that, while she . . ."

"Doesn't seem like it matters to you two *what* she was doing. You've clearly done this before. Whether Amanda was out shopping or being killed, it's still the same thing."

"Killed?"

Bethany could have bitten her tongue off. She'd allowed her personal feelings to come into it, letting her disgust for the cheating pair cloud her mind and professionalism.

Giving Melinda the same speech she'd given Keith, instead telling her to go straight home, she managed to witness the woman's overly dramatic response for about a minute, then she chivvied her out.

"Flipping hell," Mike said.

"Jim next?"

Mike nodded. "Might as well get the injured party out of the way. Plus, the poor sod helped find DeBord. What a night he's had."

Bethany opened one door and asked Jim to come inside. He walked across the lounge slowly, as though parts of him were broken, and some undoubtedly were. A bit of his heart, a slice of his mind, his limbs heavy from shock and grief.

"Hi, Jim." She closed the door. "How are you?" It could be classed as a stupid question, but not in a situation like this. If she could find out what his state of mind was, it would help her decide how to proceed.

"Gobsmacked. Sad. Angry. Quite a few things. Amanda is . . . was . . . such a bloody nice woman, you know? She didn't deserve that bastard doing what he did."

"Which bastard are you referring to?" she asked.

"Keith. And whoever . . . oh fuck . . . whoever killed her."

"It must have been a terrible thing to deal with. Can you talk me through what happened?"

He sat on the worktop and told his story, and she listened, no interruptions. While he was recalling it so clearly, in minute detail, she didn't want to break his flow.

"Then the ambulance arrived," he said.

"Okay, let's go back to Amanda's house. You say you picked up the wine bottles from the living room rug. Do you have any idea why they might have been there?"

"No. I thought it was off at the time. That's why I took them into the kitchen." He widened his eyes. "Shit, my prints will be on them."

"That's okay, don't worry about it. Do you know of anyone who'd want to do this to Amanda?"

"I'd say Keith or Melinda, but that's just me being spiteful. They wouldn't have wanted her out of the way that much. I expect they're going to be open about their relationship now anyway. Good luck to them. I don't want Melinda back — Keith's welcome to her."

"I'm sorry you had to go through what you did tonight."

Jim shrugged. "Best I found out now, eh? God knows how long they've been carrying on. But this isn't about them or me, it's about Amanda. I don't get why anyone would do this to her. She's one of the nicest people."

They usually are. "Any reason why she didn't live with Keith?"

"Maybe she had an inkling as to what he's really like and preferred to keep her own house. Keith had a thing about Lisa a while back. Two or three years ago, before Miranda caught his eye. Kept feeling Lisa up when he thought no one was looking. Amanda might have spotted it."

"Can I just ask you all the residents' names and numbers they live at?" She glanced at Mike: *Write this down for me so I don't forget who is who.*

"There's me, obviously, Lisa Hicks, Keith Trannor, Amanda DeBord, Craig Gillan, Dee Groocock, Sarah Hodgson, and Melinda. Nash, *her* surname is. There's Sarah's Bob, they're married, then there's Lisa's sister, Jane Vanes." He provided the house numbers.

"That's ten," she said. "Isn't it a bit unusual to have so many single people in one street, only one married couple?"

He shrugged. "Hadn't really thought about it. Probably because Keith and Amanda were together, and me and Melinda. It felt like there were more couples."

"And none of you have children?"

"Keith does, but his son lives with his ex-wife. He was messing about with Amanda, and the wife found out." A light bulb seemed to switch on. "He's got a pattern going. Bet Melinda hasn't noticed. He'll be cheating on her next. Sarah and Bob have kids, but they're in their own places. Think they must be twenty and twenty-three by now."

"What's Keith's ex-wife's name?"

"Vicky."

"Any reason why you and Melinda didn't live together?"

"Nope."

"Lisa and Jane have different surnames."

"Yeah, Jane's married."

"Married but not living with her husband?"

"He works away a lot. When he does come home, Jane kips there." He scrunched his forehead up. "Just remembered. A car went past when we were out on the road with Amanda. I didn't get the make or colour, though, and you'd think I would because I watched until it went round the corner."

"Size?"

"Like an Astra."

"Dark or light?"

"Dark."

"If you think of anything else, please give me a ring." She handed him her card. "We might well speak to you again at some point, but for now we're just getting the bare bones from everyone. Go home now — and don't speak to any of the others." She explained why — *I need to see their reactions when they're told.*

Jim walked out, head bent. Mike called Dee in, and they went through the same sort of questions again.

Then Bethany had others burning to get out. "Why did you perform CPR when it was clear she was dead?"

Dee flushed a similar colour to the blood around her mouth — why hadn't she washed it off? "Because I was told to, even though I knew it wouldn't work. I was asked to check for a pulse, so I touched her neck to the side, on the bit that wasn't cut. I still got blood all over my hands." She shuddered.

"Did the officer in the living room swab them and your face?"

Dee nodded.

"Did you tell the dispatcher Amanda's throat was slit?"

"I think I said something like: *There's no point.* I can't remember saying what state she was in. Jim wouldn't have seen — he was standing back a bit, and grass hid the body. I did CPR anyway. Maybe a small part of me hoped it would work." Her eyes filled.

"Okay. Do you recall seeing Amanda leave the party to pick up more wine?"

"No, I must have been indoors getting a drink, because when I came out, she was gone. Jim told me where she was."

Dee had already explained her part in going with Jim to Amanda's. Their stories matched. So Jim and Dee were out of the frame. Keith and Melinda . . . they could have killed her then went to bed. Some people got off on the thrill of death. As for the others, well, she'd find out now.

* * *

Later, with everyone spoken to and each resident in their homes, Bethany answered a knock at Keith's front door.

Isabelle stood there. "We've come to have a nose around, just to be on the safe side."

Four SOCOs stood behind her on the path.

"Keith Trannor is upstairs," Bethany said. "Glen can stay here with you."

"Where are you off to then?" Isabelle asked.

"To get some breakfast, then we'll be back to speak to the neighbours in the street behind. You never know, someone might have noticed something."

"You lucky sod. Bring us back some bacon rolls, will you?" Isabelle pulled her suit zip down and fished about beneath it. "Here's thirty quid. I've got four of my team here, three at Amanda's, and three on the verge."

Bethany took the money. "You'll have enough for coffees as well."

"That's fab. Now, are you going to get out of our way so we can come in or what?"

Bethany laughed and stepped outside. She called for Mike, and they left the quiet close, Bethany mulling all the neighbours over.

Which one of them did it? Or was it someone else entirely?

CHAPTER FIVE

David had dozed on and off, annoyed at himself for not staying awake throughout the police interviewing the Le Huray lot. Hopefully all the neighbours in his street were out cold, and anyway, if he was seen walking down the road, they'd think he was going for his usual newspaper at the little shop or on one of his early morning walks he took from time to time. He'd changed his habits on year three, waiting for the moment they'd be to his advantage. Now, his behaviour would be classed as normal for him.

Handy.

He turned the corner at the end and walked across Dee's grass at the side of her house, then went through the gateway into the rear garden. From the position of her property, no one in Le Huray would have seen him. The homes on the other side were farther up.

At her kitchen door, he tilted the flowerpot and retrieved the spare key. He'd watched her from his bedroom during his times of learning everyone's movements, and whenever Lisa had gone round there to water the plants while Dee was on holiday, she'd used this key. Every single one of them chose the flowerpots as a hiding place.

Twats.

Inside, he closed the door and remained still, listening. Then he took his scuba helmet out of the carrier bag and put it on. It looked more like one of those used when going into a building, protecting the wearer from a gas leak or whatever. The small oxygen tank beneath his jacket wasn't heavy and didn't affect his ability to move around. There was enough in it for him to do what had to be done. Besides, he was invincible while he had it on, a hidden vindicator, righting the wrongs. The only problem was, he couldn't hear anything but his breathing.

Stealth was his friend while he walked through the ground floor, checking the kitchen, lounge, utility, and little loo. Dee must be in bed. He went upstairs, using the outside of each step — less chance of them creaking.

Her bedroom door was open, and she rested on her side, facing the window. A low-watt lamp gave off a peachy glow. Had she been scared before she'd fallen asleep, thinking someone might be out to get her, too, so she'd kept the light on?

I'm out to get you.

He stood next to her bed, staring down at her, a rush of endorphins scouring his blood. He'd kill her with kindness, to match his view of her. She *was* kind. She was the nice one of the group, who cared for the others and always made sure they had food, so they didn't get too drunk.

He took his murder tools out of the bum bag that sat against his right hip. Opened it all and placed it on her nightstand. Who would have thought such things could kill, eh? But they would.

David collected Dee's belts which hung from the handle of her wardrobe door and placed them with the weapons. Holding the corner of her quilt, he peeled it back slowly. She didn't stir, probably exhausted from all that partying and alcohol. Convenient for him, deadly for her. Had she woken, she'd see him, and the helmet was sure to shit the life out of her. He'd enjoy soaking up her reaction and wished he could witness her terror for a while, but for now, with the police in Le Huray, he'd be better off doing this quickly.

He managed to tie her wrists and ankles without her rousing. Then, taking two weapons, he inserted them into her nostrils. It took some doing, what with the skin needing to give to accommodate the intrusions, but there, he'd done it, and her mouth automatically opened so she could breathe. Amazing what the body did while you were out of it. How it knew what to do. How it helped David with the next step.

She moved then, wafting her bound hands about near her face, as though batting a fly. He stared at her, at how silly she appeared with cocktail sausages plugging her nose. Then he took the four triangle quarters of grated cheese sandwiches and stuffed them in her mouth, right to the back, clogging her throat. While her eyes snapped open, he crammed in a whole scotch egg, her lips stretched around it, then pressed his gloved hand over her mouth and nose for good measure. She thrashed around, desperate for air, and he smiled at the fact he had plenty coming in through his mouthpiece. Her fists drummed her stomach, the heels of her feet the mattress, and with staring, wild eyes, she looked at him, fear widening them, knowledge she was about to die giving them a manic glint.

He knelt on her wrists, pinning them to her gut so she couldn't lift her arms and scratch at his mask. It took perhaps two minutes of her kicking, her back arching, then she stilled, and he removed his hand. Her facial orifices holding a veritable feast, he wanted to say: *How does it feel to know your kindness killed you?*

He imagined her answering, calling him a bastard, a new Dee coming to the fore, the angry one he'd never seen. She'd be missed by those in the close, but not for long if he had his way. They all had to be gone by next weekend.

Everything was working to plan.

David checked for a pulse. Nothing.

Superb!

He left the house, locking up and replacing the key beneath the flowerpot. Removed his helmet and put it in the bag. Walked away from Le Huray, around the corner into his street. The quiet street. Not a soul in sight outside or behind windows.

Indoors, he placed his helmet and oxygen tank on the top shelf in his wardrobe, then made a cuppa. He'd need a nap to ensure he got through tomorrow. His students would be grumpy, especially on a Monday, and he'd need his wits about him to manage them. Still, he'd done it for years, and with the memories of what he'd just done, plus those regarding Amanda fuelling him, he'd be fine and dandy.

He sat in his favourite chair and stared down into Keith's. People in white overalls mooched about inside and in the garden. Police. Looking for clues. The stupid prats wouldn't find any there. David wasn't about to tell them they were wasting their time, though. It was far too enjoyable watching them do it.

Such fun. Death is a party.

* * *

"So, about that conversation we had," David said, cornering Alan down the science corridor. "Sorry if I came off a bit weird. It's just that I've been reading about it so much in the news lately, and I can't help but wonder what sends these people off on a killing spree. They were innocent children once. What ruined them? Which leads me on to the main topic I wanted to discuss, but you walked out last time before I could finish."

Alan sighed, gripping his satchel handle tighter. "What's that?"

"Is there something we could be doing in school for children like those shooters? Should we be more vigilant regarding our students' home lives? Do we have a potential mass murderer among us?" He stopped himself from laughing. "Are there signs we need to look for so we can help these kids before it gets to that stage?"

"Ah, I see where you're coming from now." Alan loosened his death grip on the satchel.

"Good. I mean, as far as we know, all our students are happy, but is that just on the outside? Are they happy because they're at school, away from home or wherever they're unhappy? Will any of them one

day feel resentful towards their classmates for not living an awful life and somehow acquire a weapon and kill them?"

"Perhaps we should speak to the head about it. If we're talking going through their files to pick up on those students we know don't have it easy and concentrating on them to start with, offering privacy for a chat or whatever, then that can only be good," Alan said.

"I knew you'd see it my way." David smiled. "Sorry if you thought I was odd earlier."

"I have to admit, you worried me for a moment there, but it's okay now I know what you were really getting at. Let me know when you've got the go-ahead on this. I quite like the idea of helping these kids."

Alan walked off, and David remained where he was, smiling.

How easy it was to fool some people.

CHAPTER SIX

With the bacon rolls and coffees handed over to Isabelle and her team, Bethany and Mike stood in the street behind Le Huray Close along with Tammy Hill, one of the new uniforms, and Greg Underby, who Bethany had filched from Keith Trannor's.

"Show Tammy the ropes on door-to-door, will you?" Bethany said to Glen, smiling at Tammy. "You two take one side, me and Mike will do the other."

Bethany walked away, Mike beside her. There weren't many homes, maybe thirty, so she suggested they split up. Knocking at eight on a Sunday morning wasn't ideal, but standing outside a grotty burger van buying bacon rolls hadn't been wonderful either. She hadn't fancied those McDonald's breakfast bap things, and the van had been the only other thing open so early. Still, they'd filled a hole, and the coffee was passable, but she wished she'd opted for a McMuffin now. The bread roll sat heavy in her tummy, and the bacon grease coated her tongue.

She rapped on the first door, waiting a while for whoever lived inside to open up. Guilt at disturbing perhaps their only day for a lie-in weighed heavy on her shoulders, but with a killer out there, she had to push those thoughts aside and get the hell on with her job. Ruining people's day wasn't her main concern.

A woman answered with messy hair and a crumpled cheek from her pillow, and a line down the middle from a fabric crease. Her lilac pyjama shorts and vest top appeared new, probably bought because of the recent heat. Who wanted to get hot and bothered in their usual stuff?

"Sorry to disturb you, but I'm DI Bethany Smith, and I need to ask a couple of questions. Your name is?" She showed her ID then slid it back in her pocket.

"Elaine Wilson." She blinked, maybe from being woken, maybe from the sun, which was already bright and cheerful, the complete opposite of this woman, who looked like she wanted to tell Bethany to fuck right off and come back later. "I need coffee. Can't function." She wandered off down a hallway. "You want to stand out there or what?"

Bethany took that as the green light to go inside, so she entered and closed the door, joining Elaine in the trendy white kitchen. The woman, busy with a pod machine, stood side-on to Bethany.

"Do you want one?" Elaine mumbled, knuckling her eyes and letting out a yawn while liquid spurted into her cup.

The aroma was tempting. "No, thank you." She could do with a decent coffee, but there were too many people to speak to, and sipping a hot brew while the others chatted to the neighbours didn't seem right.

"Saves me the hassle, begging your pardon and all that," Elaine said. "I tell you, I'm fit for nothing until I've had my coffee, and seeing as I had little sleep — *again* — I'm bloody knackered. Why are you here so chuffing early?"

Bethany leant on the doorframe while Elaine added milk to her drink, then sipped with her eyes closed, as if it was the best thing she'd ever tasted. After a few more gulps, she appeared rather more with it.

Hiding a smile, Bethany asked, "I apologise for the hour. How come you didn't get much sleep?"

"That lot round the back. Noisy sods." She grabbed a bag of bread and slipped a slice in a toaster.

The party? "What about them?"

"They get together every Saturday night during the summer, even when it rains. Yep, the bleedin' marquee comes out then, and they sit underneath it, getting pissed up. Last night they did a karaoke."

Nice. "Every Saturday?"

Elaine chugged down more coffee. Swallowed. Nodded. "Without fail. Six years this has been going on, and if you ask them to tone it down a bit, you get abuse. It's like they're in a bubble and don't think about the other neighbours." She took butter out of the fridge, then a knife from a drawer.

"Have you called the police?"

"Yes, and, God love them, they come out, but it makes no difference."

"The environmental health department?"

"Well, that's my next step — *after* I record how loud they are, so I have proof or whatever. I don't want to get fobbed off, but if there's evidence, they can't ignore me, can they? Honestly, the noise level is ridiculous, and they don't give a shit, those people. Anyway, that's by the by. What did you want to ask me?"

The toast popped, hardly browned, and Elaine set about loading the knife with butter.

"It's to do with the party, actually," Bethany said.

"Ooh, I could scream. Why does butter always rip the bread? Does my nut in." She went on as though she hadn't asked a question. "So you're going to do something about it, the get-togethers?" She drank some more coffee. "This stuff saves my life. Aren't you a bit of a high rank to be bothering about parties?" Toast buttered, with a gaping hole in the middle, she took a bite. "Do you want some?"

"No, but thanks for offering." Bethany wanted to laugh. This lady was a bright spot in her otherwise horrible day. "It's not the actual party itself I'm investigating. Did you hear anything, other than the party last night, that you felt was odd?"

Elaine laughed. A crumb took up residence at the corner of her mouth, and she brushed it away. "You can't hear sod all when they're having a whale of a time. Well, apart from the neighbours in this street shouting for them to shut up. It really does mess with you for days afterwards. You know, you're tired, get arsey, and you're only feeling human again by about Wednesday. Then Saturday comes round, and the process starts all over again. You long for autumn, know what I mean?"

"I can imagine. Did you happen to nose out of your back windows?"

"No. I got my Kindle out last night. Better to read and get lost in another world than listen to the real one when they're intent on having loud fun. Some bloke was singing oldies. You know, The Righteous Brothers, that kind of thing. At one point he warbled that Gloria Gaynor song, and I muttered that he wouldn't survive if he kept singing it for much longer. You get frustrated to the point that anger takes over."

"Have you ever confronted any of them?"

"I went down the alley and shouted through the fence once. Got to be about three years ago now. One of the women told me to fuck off."

Charming. "Who was that?"

"Lisa Hicks."

"Is she usually so outspoken?" Bethany hadn't got that impression when she'd talked to her. Lisa had been quiet and polite. "If you even know her to make a comparison, that is."

"I know her from keep fit. Been going for years. She's in my class. I don't speak to her, though, just see her there. And get this, after I'd had a go and she'd said that, she *smiled* at me in the supermarket. Now, there's taking the piss, then there's taking the piss." She munched more toast.

"So you're annoyed with her, are you?" Could this woman have had enough and gone round there, bumped into Amanda while she'd been on the way to collect more wine, and lost the plot?

"I'm annoyed with the lot of them. Selfish, that's what they are. Why, is it a crime to be dogged off now?"

Bethany went for the shock reaction. "One of the party members was murdered last night."

Elaine's cup fell from her hand and smacked onto the floor. It didn't break, but the remainder of her coffee spilt on the grey lino in the shape of a candy cane. Her toast followed, slapping butter-side down. "Oh, fuck me." She grabbed a tea towel and knelt to wipe up the mess. "Murdered? Who the bloody hell would want to do that?" She got up and dumped the cup and towel in the washing-up bowl, the toast in the bin. "I know they're a pain in the arse, but killing one of them is a bit much, isn't it?"

Interesting. "So you think someone might have been *that* angry they resorted to murder?"

Elaine pressed a hand to her heart. Butter from her finger seeped into her top. "Really? Come on now. Murder is going way too far. Yes, they're inconsiderate and all that, but no, I can't see someone going down that route."

"Do you know all your neighbours?"

"Most of them, and they're not into bumping people off, I can assure you." Her breaths came out ragged. "This has shocked me a bit. I need to sit down." She staggered to a chair in the dining area. "What should I do?"

"What do you mean?"

"Well, if someone's going round killing . . ."

"Make sure you lock up at night, maybe get some extra security. A camera perhaps?"

Elaine nodded. "The retail park has that shop, doesn't it. Can't remember the name. I'll get a camera today."

"I don't feel this is someone on a spree, so to speak, so please don't worry too much."

"So it's a one-off, is that what you're saying?"

"There's never any definite answer with these things, so the camera and locking up is my advice." Bethany had to get out before the woman delayed her indefinitely. "If you hear or see anything strange, contact me right away." She handed over her card.

"I'll get my son to come and stay with me for a bit or maybe go to his." Elaine rubbed her temples. "Bleedin' Nora, murder . . ."

"Thank you for your time, and sorry if I worried you."

Goodbyes said, Bethany walked out and checked in with Mike as to who he'd spoken to in her absence. She opted for three doors down while he moved farther up. After ringing the bell, she again waited for a minute or two, then rang it a second time. If the party had been so noisy, maybe the resident was in a deep slumber. She was about to turn away and try someone else, but the rattling of a chain sliding across had her staying put.

A man stood on the threshold and, bleary-eyed, clothes skew-whiff as though he'd quickly slung them on to open the door, he gave a querying smile.

She held up her ID. "DI Bethany Smith. I just need to ask a couple of questions. Your name, sir?"

"David Chesterfield. How can I help you?"

His politeness stunned her for a second, as did his calm demeanour. "Were you home last night?"

He nodded. "Yes, marking papers."

"Oh?"

"I'm a teacher." He smiled.

"Didn't the party disturb you?"

"With it being directly behind mine, yes, it can disturb me, but once I'm into the marking, everything gets tuned out. Why, have they finally been warned properly to keep it down?"

Bethany ignored that. "Did it keep you awake when you went to bed?"

"It always does, but you get used to it and tend to drift off eventually."

"What time did you go to bed?"

"Hmm." He pressed a fingertip to his cheek. "About eleven. Managed to drop off about midnight."

Shit, that wasn't any good to her. "Did you happen to wake up?"

"Sorry, no, not until about six."

"So did you see or hear anything going on at the party before you went to bed? A row, perhaps?"

"I did hear someone singing awfully, lots of laughter, but other than that, it sounded like their usual gathering."

Elaine's comment about someone killing because of the parties prompted her to say, "How do you feel about the noise level?"

He shrugged. "What can you do? Many people have asked them to behave over the years, and they carry on. I just mind my own business, continue with my plans."

"Plans?"

"I mean living my life. You can't allow people like them to get to you, can you."

"No, I suppose not. So you didn't see anyone around who shouldn't have been?"

"I didn't look out at all, so no. Why, has something happened?"

"Thank you for your time." She wasn't about to repeat what she'd told Elaine. She should have kept that to herself, and anyway, Elaine might gossip, and David would find out soon enough.

"You're welcome," he said.

She strode away, conscious of him watching her, maybe wondering what the devil was going on. A glance back over her shoulder showed he wasn't there anymore, so the sense of being stared at must have been her imagination playing up. She shrugged and continued questioning two more residents, who complained about the noise last night, but other than that, all was normal.

At the fifth door, an elderly lady with meringue-like hair informed her she'd seen and heard nothing last night — "Ear plugs are a Godsend, dear!" — but she had spotted Mrs Omar from twenty-seven taking her pug for a walk around five-thirty this morning. Bethany thanked her and crossed the road. Glen and Tammy were still up the other end, so she knocked at twenty-seven, greeted by a woman in a teal leotard of all things, a pink towelling headband catching the sweat on her forehead.

Bethany introduced herself. "Sorry to trouble you, but a neighbour said she saw you out with your dog earlier this morning. Where did you go?"

Omar, around sixty, flapped her hand in front of her face. "Been doing a workout. Phew! Okay, I went down there." She pointed to the street opening. "I crossed over and went on towards the roundabout by the main road. There's a field. Puggy had a tiddle and a number two, then I came back."

"What time was this?"

"Always five-thirty. Puggy has a body clock that never changes. He wakes me at five-fifteen, and I usually nip out with him in my pyjamas. No one around to see me, and at my age, you just don't care, my love. You'll discover that once you're older."

"How long were you out for?"

"Back by quarter to six. I don't hang about in the mornings. After lunch is the walk where I get to properly stretch my legs."

"Did you see anything on the main road?" Bethany doubted it, seeing as it curved before the roundabout and the tent wouldn't be visible from where Omar had been, but there was no harm in asking.

"Too busy drinking my coffee. I take a to-go cup."

"Did you see anyone else?"

"No."

"What about last night? Was anyone in this street who shouldn't have been?"

"I wouldn't know. I'm tucked up by nine. Puggy likes an early night."

It sounded like Puggy ruled the bloody roost. "Do the parties bother you?" Not that she thought this woman was the killer.

"I used to live in Italy, you know, and everyone there had parties. You learn to adapt."

"Do you know if it bothers other people?"

Omar nodded. "Most of the residents along here have complained about it at some time or other. I can understand that, especially those with children. Still, they all plod on. It's what you do, isn't it?"

Bethany agreed and left her to finish her workout. She walked along to meet up with Glen and Tammy, telling them not to bother with twenty-seven. "Got anything so far?"

Glen shook his head. "Nothing up the far end — they don't tend to hear the party noise that badly, and everyone was asleep at the time of the murder."

"How long left of your shift?" she asked him. "You must be knackered."

Glen shrugged. "Another four hours. I finish at twelve — started at two."

She turned her attention to Tammy. "And how are you finding being a copper?"

"Love it," she said. "This is my first week in Shadwell. I moved here from Bicester."

"Oh, Oxfordshire?"

Tammy nodded. "My boyfriend, Charlie, got a job up this way, so it made sense for me to work here, too."

"How long have you been on the force?"

"Four years."

"Brilliant. Right, you two carry on this side. I'm off to see Mike."

She jogged over the road and waited for him at someone's gate. He finished with the resident and met her on the path.

"Sod all," he said. "I've got one house left. You coming with me?"

"May as well." She quickly told him what she'd found out.

"Blimey, good job the Omar woman wasn't taking dear Puggy out much earlier. She could have been dead if she had."

"Indeed. Scary thought, although perhaps she wouldn't have been if Amanda was targeted and not a random kill."

"Hmm. Come on. Let's get this one over with, then we can help the other two on their side."

CHAPTER SEVEN

At the final door, Mike knocked hard. A man appeared from the side of the house, his trousers dirty on the knees. Bethany's warning alert went off — could he be burying something? The weapon? She introduced them, and they flashed their IDs.

"What's your name, sir?" Bethany asked.

"Eion Watts. Can you come round the back?" he asked. "Only, I want to get the flowers planted so I can take the missus to breakfast."

Was he acting this way to throw them off, inviting them to the place where he was hiding evidence?

"There's that new café that opened," Eion said. "All Day Grub. You heard of it?"

"No, can't say I have," Bethany answered.

They followed him into the rear garden. A row of large black ceramic flowerpots stood side by side on the patio, bags of soil and plants in plastic trays in front. She scanned the rest of the area — just grass, no flowerbeds, nothing dug up as far as she could see. A hedge at the bottom, trimmed nicely, a sapling in the centre surrounded by a circle of pebbles, filled in with white gravel slightly discoloured with algae or whatever the hell that green stuff was.

Eion grabbed an open soil bag and poured some into a pot. "What can I do you for?" He glanced across and grinned. "Or have you come to do me for something? I'm sure my car is taxed, and I haven't mugged anyone lately."

Bethany smiled. *I hope he's bloody joking.* "Just a few questions. Do the parties down the way bother you? I heard they've been going on for years."

"Bloody bothered me last night, I can tell you." He moved on to filling the other pots. "Ended up gobbing off out the window, didn't I."

"Gobbing off in what way?"

"Told them to shut up, that there's people trying to sleep. It never works, but I do the same thing every time. I think it's to get some anger out, know what I mean?"

"What sort of anger?"

Eion paused and stared at her as if she were stupid. "Being pissed off at not getting to sleep, that sort of anger."

"Did you shout from your window or go down there?"

"From the window." He indicated above. "They laughed and carried on. It was karaoke last night, so it's worse when they do that. If it's just their chatter and music, it doesn't grate so much." He put the bag down and picked up a tray of flowers, plonking his arse on a wooden bench, then leant forward to plant.

"What time did you shout?" she asked.

"Three minutes past two — I know that because I looked at the clock and got rattled about it." He positioned a flower in the soil then pressed around it to pack it in.

"Did you happen to see anything going on at the main road?" Her heart rate went a bit mental at the idea he might have clocked something.

"No, I was too busy staring down at the party. You can see their house from up there." He jerked a thumb at the sky. "They had all the lights on and were out in the garden. All right, there are hedges and whatever at the ends of some gardens down this row, but I can still see them getting drunk." He popped another flower in. "Honestly, it really does get your goat and makes you feel like you're an old moaner. I love a party myself, but not at the expense of upsetting the neighbours."

"Did you hear anything other than the party?"

"Nope. I got back in bed, shoved a pillow over my head, and finally got to sleep."

"You mentioned your wife. Did she get out of bed?"

"She'd sleep through a hurricane, she would. Didn't even wake when I shouted."

"Okay, well, thank you for talking to us, Eion. Your pots are going to look lovely, by the way. Enjoy your breakfast." *More than I enjoyed mine.*

"Cheers."

Bethany and Mike left the garden and met up with Glen and Tammy to sort out the last few houses. With no more information from the remaining residents, the uniforms went off to the next street with instructions to contact Bethany if they got anything useful. Bethany led the way across the road and went down the alley beside David Chesterfield's, striding through into Le Huray Close.

Isabelle was just leaving Keith Trannor's place. "He's still asleep, that Keith. And we've finished in there. I left him a note to let him know what we've done — fingerprinting and whatnot — and we'll do his room later when he gets up. Is Glen coming back?"

"If you need him, get hold of him. He's currently with another unit doing house-to-house."

"No, I don't need him, was just asking so he didn't knock on this door and disturb Keith. Tory and Nicola can get going now." Isabelle called over and told them to leave. "The body has been removed, and I've got three of my team checking beneath where Amanda was, then we're done." Her face lit up as though she'd remembered something. "Where did you get those breakfast rolls from? Talk about nasty bacon."

"I do apologise," Bethany said haughtily, smiling. "I didn't realise you were into cordon bleu butties."

"Come on, you have to admit they were rank."

"I'm admitting nothing. Conveniently, we're off now. I need to get Fran and Leona in to do all the usual searches."

"Poor things, giving up their Sunday." Isabelle swiped at her brow like some bint on a fainting couch.

Bethany watched Tory and Nicola drive away. "You're a silly sod, Izz. Did you get any idea how long digi forensics will be with Amanda's laptop and phone?"

"Your guess is as good as mine."

"Okay, see you when I see you."

"Hopefully not too soon," Isabelle said. "Love you, but I don't want to see you for at least another month."

Bethany gave her the middle finger and walked over to where she'd left her car outside one of the houses. Once they were seated, she said to Mike, "Let's draw a map of this street and write down who lives where on it. There are too many people to keep track of."

Mike did that while she rang Fran and Leona. They'd be going to the station now to begin the laborious task of checking Amanda's social media and activities, as well as the other residents.

Lisa Hicks came out of number six and crossed the close, going down the side of number one. She looked knackered.

"She hasn't slept long." Bethany nodded at the woman. "Who lives at number one?"

Mike stared down at his notebook. "Dee."

"Righty-oh. Pissing heck, it's hot already." She started the engine and lowered her window. "Changing the subject . . . The bacon wasn't *that* bad, was it?"

Mike huffed out a laugh and popped his notebook and pen away. "It wasn't the best."

"Better than nothing, though," she grumbled, then remembered her own thoughts on the food. "All right, I admit it, they were manky. So, we'll go to the station, properly brief Fran and Leona, write things up on the whiteboards, then go from there, yes?"

A female scream rang out, long and filled with fright, followed by another, which was hoarser, broken.

"Who the fuck was *that*?" Bethany cut the engine and leapt out onto the pavement.

Mike did the same and stood in the road, while Isabelle came flying through the hedge by the semicircle of grass, heading towards them. Then Mike was off, legging it to Dee's.

"I'll get Tory and Nicola back," Isabelle said, phone to her ear. "And oi, I said I didn't want to see you for another month!"

Bethany ignored her and followed Mike. There was a time and place for jokes, and she was too keyed up to see the funny side. Mike was nowhere in sight, so she rushed to enter the garden. A flowerpot had been moved, revealing a crescent of damp on the patio slab, and the door stood open.

"Oh God, oh my bloody God!" Lisa Hicks. Panicked. Scared.

"Mike?" Bethany called up the stairs.

"Up here. Get Isabelle!"

She dashed back out into the street, her guts going south, and called, "Mike asked for you to come. Might want to get your team to wait."

"Shit, there's only three of mine left here; I sent the others home. Give me a minute or so to tell them." Isabelle darted off towards the hedge.

Bethany returned to the house and climbed the stairs. On the landing, she got her bearings. Three closed doors, one open. She headed for that, adrenaline swaggering through her, and stopped by the frame, her breathing heavy.

She stared at the bed for a second, then at Mike, who shook his head: *She's dead.*

Jesus Christ.

"Okay, out," Bethany said. They needed protective clothing on, and Lisa shouldn't be here.

Mike put his arm around a sobbing Lisa and guided her downstairs. With another glance into the bedroom, Bethany sighed. *What the fucking hell?*

She met up with Mike and Lisa in the back garden, then led the way out into Le Huray.

"Take her home," she said to Mike. "I'll be with you in a sec."

He gently tugged Lisa, and Bethany looked over at the main road hedge. Isabelle and a SOCO came through the gap, and they hurried to her.

"What the chuff is going on?" Isabelle asked.

"You'll need a fresh team." Bethany grimaced and lowered her voice. "Dee Groocock is sodding dead."

"What?" Isabelle's eyes widened. "Okay" — she turned to the SOCO — "new gear on, please."

"The back door's open, so you have access." Bethany gazed across at the mouth of the close. "Ah, here's Tory and Nicola." She walked over and waited for them to park.

Isabelle and the SOCO dipped back through the hedge.

With the officers out of the car, Bethany said quietly, "Tory, do your usual at the back door of number one."

"Seriously?" Tory's eyebrows shot up.

"Unfortunately, yes. Nicola, you stand at the front so no other neighbours get the idea to go down there. Make sure you can see the whole close." Bethany turned to Tory. "Did you spot anyone leaving their homes before you left?"

Tory frowned. "No one entered the street in vehicles or on foot either."

"Okay, so we're looking at someone who doesn't live here, or someone on Dee's side of the street climbing over the back fences to get to hers. In Le Huray, those in the frame for that are Keith at number four, Jim at three, Craig at two. Christ Almighty! Listen, I have to go and speak to the neighbour who found her — Lisa Hicks — so if you need me, you know where I am."

She left them to it, messaging Fran to let her know of the hold up and what it was about, then entered number six, the door left ajar. She found Mike and Lisa in an ultra-modern red kitchen, Lisa sitting at the breakfast bar, a turquoise blanket around her, Mike sorting tea.

Bethany sat beside Lisa, the stool a bit too high for her liking. While the kettle chugged to life, Mike took his notebook and pen out. He nodded at Bethany to crack on.

"Lisa, I'm so sorry you had to witness that. Can I ask what you were doing at Dee's?"

Lisa turned her watery eyes to Bethany. "I was . . . I had to wake her up. We were meant to be going to . . . to see . . . see the lions."

"And where is that?"

"The wildlife park. Our coach leaves at eleven."

Well, they'll be bloody missing that. "The wildlife park up the road?"

Lisa nodded.

"So you went there to wake her up. Even though you'd both had very little sleep, and after what had happened to Amanda, you were still going out for the afternoon?"

Lisa blinked. "I . . . we agreed to go anyway. Amanda would have wanted us to."

"That's nice." *Did that sound sarcastic?* "How did you get into Dee's?"

Mike poured boiled water into three cups — it must have already been hot, maybe from Lisa having a cuppa before she'd left. Bethany could hug him. She needed something to get the taste of that greasy bacon out of her mouth.

Lisa sob-hiccoughed. "We all leave keys under flowerpots."

That explained the one in Dee's garden being moved.

"Is that common knowledge to anyone else?" Bethany asked. "As in, people who don't live in the close?"

"I don't know. I've never told anybody."

Mike placed cups on the bar. Bethany pulled Lisa's forward, encouraging her to drink. Bethany blew her own and sipped. Tetley, had to be.

Giving Lisa a moment to calm herself, Bethany thought about the keys. Anyone in those gardens backing onto Keith's could have heard them discussing their whereabouts. Any number of the close residents could have mentioned it to family, friends and colleagues. The thing was, Elaine's comment about someone being arsey about the parties was growing legs. Two people in the same street, dead?

Bethany couldn't afford to discount it, especially since Tory hadn't seen anyone leaving their homes — but that didn't mean they hadn't. All the people Bethany had spoken to in the houses behind had been nice. She'd have to ask Mike if he'd got any dodgy feelings about the ones he'd talked to, but surely he'd have said if he had, as would Glen. But what about Tammy? Being new around here, she might not have had the courage to speak up to a DI. Bethany would have to chat to her, see if the young uniform had picked up on something Glen may have missed.

"Are you all right to proceed?" she asked Lisa.

"No, but I have to, don't I?"

"I'm afraid so. Tell me what happened."

Lisa sniffed. "I crossed the road and walked down the side of Dee's. Opened her gate. Got the key out. She hadn't been answering my messages or calls, so I thought it best to go to her house. I stepped inside, called out, but she didn't respond, so I went straight upstairs. Found her . . . found her . . . like . . . that." More tears came, and she put her cup down and covered her face with both hands.

"Take your time." Bethany drank some tea.

Lisa dragged her hands down her face and then folded them on the bar. "I screamed. I mean, that *food*. What had she *done*? Choked to death?"

No, she hadn't bloody killed herself by deliberately choking, unless she really had stuffed whatever it was up her nose and crammed what Bethany thought was a scotch egg in her mouth. She flushed out the image of the cracked breadcrumb-and-sausage coating, the white of the egg showing through, lips stretched around it.

It didn't make sense to commit suicide that way. Women tended to go for pills coupled with alcohol, or exsanguination — slitting the wrists to drain the blood. Men often opted for hanging and asphyxia — plastic bags over their heads. Bethany had never heard of anyone using food as the method, although women did tend to be more creative.

"What happened then?" Bethany prodded.

"I screamed again, I think, and I wanted to touch her wrist to check for a pulse, but I couldn't. I was scared and just stood there, bloody useless."

"Don't beat yourself up about that. No one knows how they'll react in that situation. The fear of a dead body is very real and frightening. Did you end up touching her at all?"

"No. I . . . No."

"That's good. What then?"

"He came in and took the pulse." She looked over at Mike.

Bethany held Lisa's hand. "Remember when I questioned you earlier? I asked if you knew of anyone who would want to hurt Amanda. Do you know who would want to do this to Dee?"

Lisa lost her breath on a sob. "No! They're my friends. I can't . . . I don't understand what's happening. What's going on?"

I'd like to know the same thing. "As two people in your street have been murdered, someone clearly has an issue. Did they have mutual friends or acquaintances?"

"They both work for the council." Lisa wiped her face with her sleeve.

Ah, a lead? "The same department?"

"No. Amanda is in council tax, Dee in housing benefit."

Well, that could be any number of pissed-off people. No one liked paying their council tax, and housing benefit weren't known for pulling their fingers out of their arses and getting a move on with claims. Once, in her uniform days, Bethany had been called out to a home where people were being evicted through no fault of their own, just that their rent hadn't been paid owing to housing benefit not coughing up in time. She'd had to defuse the situation by explaining to the landlord, and thankfully, the crisis had passed. A week later, the rent had been settled in full, but in the meantime, the family had had the extra worry on their shoulders on top of the husband losing his job.

"So you've never heard them discussing work colleagues?" Bethany sipped her drink. "Any spats, disagreements?"

"Not that I remember."

"Okay, do you have someone who can come and sit with you, preferably not a neighbour as we'll need to speak to them next."

"My sister. She's in bed. Jane."

"We'll quickly talk to her before we leave."

That sorted, and Jane providing nothing of use, Bethany and Mike exited the house and closed the door. They went over to Nicola, who stood with her hands behind her back, looking all important, bless her.

"Any movement from other residents?" Bethany glanced up and down the close.

"No. A new lot of SOCO have gone in, though," Nicola said.

Bethany spotted the van parked across the close entrance, blocking half the road. A police cordon had been put up, tied to the lampposts. "Right, well, we need to speak to the other neighbours now, plus I need to get hold of Glen." She gave him a ring. "Hi. Everything going okay?"

"Yes, thank you. Nothing to report as yet."

"Can you put Tammy on, please?"

"Yep."

A shuffle of the phone changing hands, then a tentative, "Hello?"

"Hi, it's Bethany Smith, the DI."

"Yes?"

"Nothing to worry about. When you were with Glen, questioning the neighbours in the previous street, did you notice whether anybody was off? Like, shifty?"

"No, they were all really nice."

"Thanks. I'll let you get on." She pocketed her phone. To Mike, "Come on, fella. Off we go."

After another hour waking everyone up and asking questions, they were no closer to finding anything out. They'd all been asleep, which wasn't surprising, given the amount of drink they'd imbibed. Every one of them expressed immense shock at the news of Dee's passing, and all the while, Bethany kept asking herself: *Which one of you fuckers did it?*

CHAPTER EIGHT

David couldn't stop laughing. The sound of Lisa bloody Hicks screaming had told him all he needed to know. She'd found that Dee woman. He'd gone upstairs to nose out from behind a partially closed curtain after those detectives had been and gone. It had been worth the wait to listen to Lisa's distress. Her going inside Dee's had sent adrenaline rushing through him, and he'd held his breath, counting one, two, three . . . four, five, six . . . eleven, twelve, thirteen . . . shriek!

Hahaha. Ahahaha.

It wasn't long before that man copper had barrelled in after her, then the woman. God, to be a fly on the wall. What had they thought when they'd spotted Dee with all that food in her mouth? And the cocktail sausages . . .

Ahahaha.

He was going to do himself some damage if he didn't stop laughing. He was finding it difficult to catch his breath.

"Stop it now," he said, as if a stern talking to would sort him out.

Instead, it made things worse.

Giggling like a loon, he nipped downstairs to make a coffee, then returned to his window spot. A few of those white-suited people had gone in after the detectives had left with Lisa, and some ginger man had entered, also in a white suit. He'd stood in the doorway, lifting his hood, then wrote something on what David thought was a tablet that a uniformed officer held out.

This was better than anything on TV.

Ah, those coppers were back. The man and woman. They had their hoods down, too, and raised them after writing on the tablet, then stepped inside. David got his binoculars out and trained them on the back bedroom. Dee's. He had no fear of the sun glinting off the lenses as it was currently sitting pretty behind his house.

LOL, as the kids at school would say. Even Mother Nature was on his side.

What a lovely bitch.

CHAPTER NINE

Presley popped his clipboard away as Bethany and Mike, suited up, entered Dee's bedroom. It seemed smaller now, what with herself, Mike, Presley, Isabelle, the photographer, and a SOCO crammed in. The poor woman on the bed . . . Bethany felt awful that so many of them crowded round while she was in such a state.

Now there was more time, Bethany studied Dee. What the hell was that up her nose? Surely it wasn't mini sausages, was it? Dee's eyes bulged, and petechiae marred her cheeks, especially the area beneath her lower lashes. She had definitely choked on that food. Her wrists were tied with a belt. Her ankles, too.

"A hand was clamped over her nose and mouth," Presley said. "Finger and thumb print bruising while she was alive — much pressure was applied."

The startling image of Dee's head being pressed so far into the pillow that it all but obscured her face flashed through Bethany's mind. She hated these visuals, hated her brain more for conjuring them.

"Bruises on the backs of the wrists," Presley went on, "indicative of her being held down, possibly with a knee, an elbow at a push. I say a knee because it's larger and spans both wrists and fits the shape. With a hand on her face as well, she wasn't going anywhere and had no chance at fighting if the person was strong. Suffocation via food. Now, I've dealt with choking victims before, but this is deliberate and is a first for me."

Bethany shuddered. Having choked a couple of times herself, nothing serious, and still being able to breathe through her nose, that had been bad enough, but to have *all* access to oxygen removed? Christ, Dee must have been panicked and scared out of her wits.

"This is bloody awful," she said. "What, did the killer grab food from the party, knowing they were going to kill her this way?"

"It's a possibility we have to consider," Mike said. "We'll need to question what food was on offer."

"There are no cocktail sausages or scotch eggs in her fridge," Isabelle said. "No packaging in the bin either, although we haven't checked the outside wheelie bin yet."

The photographer gave a wave and left the room.

"Get that grub out of her mouth, Pres," Isabelle said. "I'll hold the tubs." She grabbed a few plastic ones from a cardboard box out on the landing, then came and stood beside Presley.

He did as asked, removing the scotch egg carefully, although the coating broke further upon being placed in a tub. "There's more food in here."

Bethany jolted at that. "What sort?"

"Looks like bread to me," Isabelle said.

Presley scooped out a wodge of bread with orange flecks in it. "Cheese, I reckon." That also went into a tub. "It goes right back into her throat. Hang on." He took the rest out. "Okay, that's it. Want me to remove the things from her nose?"

Isabelle nodded and stood by with a third tub.

The sausages taken out, he used a torch and peered into her nostrils. "Nothing else is in there."

This was one of the strangest things Bethany had ever seen. It kind of beat the bugs placed in orifices that had taken place in a previous case. Food was for eating, not to kill someone with. Well, not in this way. She'd heard about a man overfeeding his wife on purpose over several years so she got diabetes. He hadn't taken her to the doctor for tests when she'd become ill, and she'd put on too much weight anyway, which had her housebound. Without insulin, she'd died, and he'd almost got away with it, too, if he hadn't bragged to a friend about what he'd done. Thankfully, Bethany hadn't had to deal with that one. It had happened in Scotland, but news sometimes filtered to different stations, incidents discussed over a cuppa in the canteen.

"Maybe the killer just grabbed the food as a means to murder her with," Mike suggested. "She could have annoyed someone at the party, the random thought of her choking on the sandwiches had gone through their mind, and it went from there."

"I prefer that to thinking someone actually planned this," Bethany said. "Because that's just damn creepy, sitting there thinking of ways to kill someone. And if it's the same person who offed Amanda, why didn't they use the blade on her? Why not just come in here and slit Dee's throat as well?"

"Hmm." Mike folded his arms. "Maybe the knife used — or the sword, whatever — was too obvious to bring here if someone was watching, or too big when climbing over garden fences. What time of death are we talking?" He cocked his head at Presley.

"Two secs." Presley inserted the temperature tool into Dee's ear. "Bear in mind with the weather and it being hot . . ."

"Yep, it could change the timings," Bethany said. "A roundabout estimate will do. We know she was alive near five because we questioned her then sent her home. She had time to get her pyjamas on, climb into bed, maybe go to sleep."

Presley nodded. "Between five and seven a.m."

"Right, so at fiveish we were still at Keith's. Later, we would have been going to get the breakfast." Bethany couldn't remember the time they'd left Keith's to collect the food. *Fuck it.* She'd have to check the log. "So, if we were at Keith's, whoever this was came here and committed murder with the police around. Shitting heck, they've got some balls."

"And the same goes for if we were at the burger van," Mike said. "Tory was right over the road in plain sight, for God's sake."

"So if they didn't climb the fences from numbers two, three, or four, or they came down the alley from the street behind, whoever it was could have easily nipped along the side of the house because the grass there butts up to the footpath that leads out of the close. They could have parked, done this, and then left. Or walked. Either way, it was right under our noses. Tory wouldn't have been able to see from her position outside Amanda's, which is number five."

Presley pushed Dee onto her side and peered at the bedsheet. "Surely Tory would have spotted headlights. The beams would have been visible." He placed her back down.

"I thought that," Isabelle said. "But it's the summer. The sun comes up well early, so no headlights. But the sound of an engine . . . unless they cut that and coasted along before parking."

"So someone on foot is likely," Bethany mused. "A man or woman in this vicinity."

She thought about the Obbington case where a member of a friendship group had killed some of the others. Was this the same thing here? One of the neighbours had done it? Apart from Keith being a bit of a knobhead and Melinda waspish, they all seemed close-knit and got along. Then again, James Obbington had appeared to get along with his friends, too . . .

She sighed. "If we're talking someone local, that's one hell of a lot of houses to visit. I'll just get hold of Glen now and ask him to extend the door-to-door to a wider area. This could take *days* — and we don't have that long if someone's of a mind to murder everyone else in this fucking close."

Frustration was getting the better of her, and she rang Glen, toning her voice down a bit so he didn't think she was shitty with him. Then she contacted Rob on the front desk and asked that he made sure other uniforms took off where

Glen and Tammy finished once their shift was over, plus to send more out to cover the whole estate.

"We'd best find out what food was served," she said. "Bye for now."

She exited, her heart heavy, and tromped down the stairs, into the garden, taking off her outer gear. Mike at her side, she signed the log, waved at Tory, and then walked up to Nicola. "Any movement?"

"Nothing."

"Okay."

In the middle of the street, she contemplated who to ask about the snacks at the party. Recalling everyone she'd spoken to, she opted for Jim Ody at number three. He opened the door with a resigned expression and ushered them inside. While they didn't need to discuss it indoors, the fewer people who could listen in, the better, then she told herself the point was moot. He'd probably tell the others what was asked.

His lounge was the same layout as Keith's, although the double doors to the kitchen were closed. Bethany and Mike took a seat on the cream velvet sofa, while Jim flopped onto a black leather beanbag — massive thing, it was.

"Sorry to trouble you yet again today when you're going through grief," Bethany said, "but can you remember what food was at the party?"

"What's the food got to do with anything?" he asked, eyebrows drawn down.

She may as well tell him. Lisa probably would. "Dee was choked to death with it."

"What?" He shot up off the beanbag. "So she wasn't murdered?"

"Oh yes, she was murdered. I won't go into details, so could you please try to recall what everyone ate?"

"Well, there were Dee's sandwiches. Always grated cheese and cut into triangles."

Oh God . . .

"Then there were the usual cocktail sausages — Melinda always provides those. She can't cook so buys them ready-made.

She's the type to even fuck up beans in the microwave." He sneered at that. "Craig bought the crisps, Keith the Twiglets, and Jane made some lovely scotch eggs from scratch. It's the same stuff we have at every party. Oh, Sarah and Bob brought chocolate cupcakes this time instead of vanilla."

Bethany hadn't been able to tell if the scotch egg in Dee's mouth had been homemade, but no matter, all the food used to kill her had been available at the party. That was all she needed to know. "Thank you. We'll leave you be now." She rose.

"Wait." Jim held out a hand in a gesture to stop her from walking out. "Are you saying someone at the *party*, one of my *friends*, killed her?"

"I'm not saying anything of the sort," she said.

"But it's likely, yes?" he pressed.

"It's likely." What was the point in trying to hide it? He wasn't stupid. Two plus two was four in this case.

"Bugger me," he said. "I can't get my head around this. I'd swear *none* of us would do it. We're all too close."

"Well, someone had a problem with Amanda and Dee. Two friends don't get murdered for no reason. We must get on. As you can appreciate, there's lots to do."

She showed herself out and called to Nicola, "We'll be at the station for a bit."

Nicola nodded, and Bethany plonked herself into the car, already exhausted in mind and body. When Mike got in, she started the engine, wishing she could unsee Dee with that food in her mouth.

I'll never eat from a buffet again without thinking of that woman.

* * *

Two whiteboards brimmed with information that Bethany and Mike had written up. The third had a few details Fran and Leona had discovered. Bethany had set Leona the task of finding out who they could contact at the council about Amanda and Dee. With it being Sunday, they were probably going to be shit out of luck.

Now she was up to date with logging information from the scenes, Bethany turned to face the others. "Fran, what did you get from social media on this lot?" She tapped the board with all the Le Huray names on it.

Fran pulled her pad across the desk to consult it. "They're all friends with each other on Facebook, although only two of them are particularly active — Melinda Nash and Craig Gillan. The others tend to drift on and off. Bob isn't on there at all — and if he is under a different name, Sarah hasn't got him listed as her husband. There are no other friends in common with any of them, so that's saved us a hell of a lot of work sifting through people. It's weird, like they're this little clique that no one else is involved with."

Bethany thought about that. "Hmm, living in the same close for years and having summer parties . . . It's clear they hang out together and class themselves as separate from others. I take it Jane Vanes is also included in that?"

Fran nodded.

"So they've taken her into the fold okay," Bethany said. "What about Sarah and Bob's kids?"

"I can't find any kids on Sarah's," Fran said. "But if they're in their twenties like you said, they're more likely not to use Facebook. None of them are on Twitter or Instagram, by the way, not that I can see. MeWe is out, too. Also curious is that Vicky Trannor, Keith's ex-wife, isn't friends with any of them. So do we assume she was unfriended once they split up and Vicky moved out? They took Keith's side? Didn't you say he'd been messing about with Amanda behind Vicky's back?"

"Maybe they thought it best to stay friends with the one who remained in the close," Bethany said. "Digi have Amanda's phone and laptop, so perhaps we'll get something from private messages. Of course, they'll also have Dee's to look through now. It might be an idea to pay this Vicky a visit to get a feel for Keith. While I don't think this is the case, Keith and Melinda could have left the house via the front, knowing no one in the close was home to see them, killed Amanda, returned to his place the same way, then went upstairs. We'll have to wait for forensics on that one. Keith's house has been gone through, so any traces of evidence will be found. Isabelle still needs to do his bedroom, though."

"Bit weird, letting Keith stay in bed while Isabelle and her lot were in there," Leona said, frowning.

"It's a delicate situation in Le Huray," Bethany said. "If Isabelle made the call for him to remain in the house, it was probably so he didn't kick up a fuss. Best he slept through it than either hang about making a nuisance of himself or pestering the other neighbours. It's her decision to answer to if it's questioned by the chief, so let's not waste time discussing that. What's done is done."

"Anyone want a coffee?" Mike asked, looking like a spare part.

Everyone nodded.

"Thanks," Bethany said to him. "Leona, anything on the council?"

She nodded. "I found out the names of Amanda's and Dee's bosses, then rang them at home. Both were happy to chat, although upset about their deaths. From what they said, Amanda and Dee were well-liked at work, had no conflicts. They'll go through both their logs tomorrow to see if anyone has threatened them or become arsey recently — the public, I mean."

"Okay. Are they contacting you, or have you got to get hold of them?"

Leona leant back, her chair creaking. "They'll ring me if something crops up."

"Right, well, there's nothing we can do about that but wait." Bethany rolled her shoulders. Stiffness was kicking in from being up so early. "Now then, we know Amanda's next of kin are on holiday, but what about Dee's?"

Leona shot forward to read her notes. "Her family live in Leeds. She hasn't married and has no children. I've contacted Leeds police. They said they'd deal with breaking the news."

"Good, that's great." Bethany sighed. "So, it's the usual digging into the family and friends of everyone, and given the amount of people involved here, it'll be a big job." Her stomach growled. Was it really lunchtime? "Okay, let's break for food. Leona, will you do the honours?" She gave her twenty quid. "A sandwich will do me, ta. I need to bugger off into my office and have a think." She accepted the coffee Mike handed her, then went into her sanctuary, not that she ever spent much time in there to appreciate it.

To get her head straight, she drew another map of Le Huray and noted the names and addresses:

1: Dee
2: Craig
3: Jim
4: Keith
5: Amanda
6: Lisa Hicks and Jane Vanes
7: Sarah and Bob Hodgson
8: Melinda Nash

She added the street behind — Casprey Lane. She recalled where Elaine Wilson, David Chesterfield, and Mrs Omar and Puggy lived, but for all the other names, she'd have to ask Mike and Glen.

"What time did Glen say he was finishing?" she muttered while prodding his number on her phone.

He answered.

"Ah, did I catch you in time?" she asked.

Glen laughed. "We're still going. Decided to put in a bit of overtime, get the second street finished. There are only four other uniforms available to help."

"Aww, you're a star. What I need you to do is tell me all the names and addresses of the people you've spoken to today."

"Righty-oh. Ready?"

"Yep."

He reeled them off, and Bethany scribbled them down on a fresh piece of paper. Call ended, she added those people to the map, then drew the current street Glen and Tammy were on, adding those names, too. She went into the incident room and passed the list to Fran.

"Can you run checks on all these, please? A fair few, I know," Bethany said. "I want any previous, mainly. Anyone in trouble, we flag them, look into them."

"Okay." Fran didn't appear the remotest bit frazzled by the request. The woman was brilliant at working fast on several different tasks.

"Is Leona out getting the nosh?"

"Yes, she nipped to the mini-mart down the road."

Bethany didn't say anything about that, but her thought? *Not another shitty meal.*

Really, she ought to get over the damn bacon from this morning.

She returned to her office and studied the map. David Chesterfield lived directly behind Keith. Now she thought about it properly, could anyone really have fence-jumped into Dee's from behind without SOCO in Keith's garden noticing? No one could have used the alley beside Keith's either — Tory would have spotted them. That left the road entrance to Le Huray. The question was, who the fuck was bold enough to just walk into Dee's when the area was heavy with police presence? Someone who knew where the key was kept . . .

Whoever it was, they had a sense of entitlement, and she aimed to find out exactly who it was and bring them down.

CHAPTER TEN

Jim Ody needed to get out. Caged in, that was what this was like. A goldfish bowl, the police out there, him in here. While he felt sick to his stomach about what had happened to his friends, he also had his head crammed with other visuals. He'd thought seeing Amanda dead or imagining Dee choking on food would have been at the forefront of his mind, but no, Melinda and Keith cavorting on the bed overtook everything.

Did that make him selfish? He struggled with that. How could he be thinking of *them* so much? Because he was hurt? Gutted?

He remembered Keith's hairy arse moving. Melinda jumping off the bed. The punch to Keith's face. Jim hoped his nose fucking hurt and never healed straight. That'd teach him. What right did those two have to do what they'd done, maybe even at the time Amanda was being murdered? The rest of them had been carrying on as usual in the garden, and if Amanda had screamed, it wouldn't have been heard because of Craig's karaoke session.

Annoyed but at the same time at a loss, Jim left his house, intent on keeping his usual appointment for a hair of the dog at The Fox and Grapes, the little pub three streets down. He usually went with Melinda for a Sunday roast, but he was fucked if he'd ask her today. Or ever. She'd chosen Keith, and Jim just couldn't get over that. Melinda *knew* what Keith had done to Vicky with Amanda, so why the hell had she let him put his pervy hands on her? What was it about the bloke that had women fawning all over him? If Jim were honest, Keith was a wanker, and Jim only tolerated him for the sake of the group, so what was the attraction?

Jim walked towards Dee's, and a shiver went through him at her body being inside. A copper stood there and nodded, hands behind her back, feet planted a foot or so apart. He had the insane urge to tell her where he was going — if someone had it out for his friends, why not him, too? Plus, he wanted her to know so they could check his alibi. For all he knew, someone could get killed while he wasn't home. Was this how it was going to be from now on? Covering his tracks, making sure people saw him so he wasn't accused?

Shit.

"I'm off to the pub," he said, staring the copper straight in the eye.

"That's fine, sir." She smiled.

"The Fox and Grapes, all right?"

"Right, sir." She gave him a funny look: *Why are you telling me this? Have you got something to hide?*

He hadn't thought of it from her point of view.

Bollocks.

Damage done, he strode out of the close, head held high, turning left, and walked past the end of Casprey Lane where that bloke lived, the weird one who didn't like them having parties.

Do you blame him?

Guilt prodded Jim, and not for the first time either. Maybe in future they ought to go inside once it got to eleven o'clock so the people in Casprey didn't hear them so much. The police had suggested that on one of their visits, but Keith was having none of it. He reckoned they could be as noisy as they bloody well liked. Keith also reckoned he could nab other people's birds an' all, and that wasn't right either.

Do I really want to go to the parties now, after what he's done, and without Amanda and Dee there?

It wouldn't be the same, would it? Then again, he'd thought that after Vicky had left Keith, yet everyone had carried on like before, and her absence wasn't felt after the first few gatherings.

Tears pricked the backs of his eyes. Fuck. While he liked Amanda well enough, he was good mates with Dee. She was a right laugh. No more, though — and Jim couldn't get his head around it. Last night, they'd been having a good time, then Amanda had gone to get her wine, and that was it, life changed forever.

He veered into the street where the pub stood bow-bellied halfway down, the bow a massive window with bull's-eyes in the small square panes, distorting the view from inside or outside. Not really fancying a drink now but desperate for some normality, something the same as what it had been before all this shit had happened, he pushed the door open.

The familiar scent of dried alcohol and various different foods smacked into him — meat, chips, maybe a bit of fish — and for a moment, he forgot everything. Until, out of habit, he turned to ask Melinda where she wanted to sit. She wasn't there, of course she wasn't, and Bob and Sarah weren't sitting up at the bar either, arses perched on red-velvet-topped stools, half a lager and lime in front of them, and let's not forget the cheese and onion Walkers.

This was all wrong.

The urge to escape came on — to run away from his thoughts, his memories, but legging it until his lungs burst wouldn't solve anything. No, the damn emotions would go with him, ripping into him, hurting, disturbing, laughing, mocking, Keith and Melinda giggling over what they'd been up to.

Jim had lost who he'd thought was the love of his life and two dear friends.

What the hell was he doing here?

He walked out onto the street, and that party-hating bloke was there, leaning on the bay window with a baseball cap peak pulled low, one leg over the other, the toe of his boot pressed to the pavement. The mad sod had all black on. *In this weather?* He held something round inside a carrier bag, and a stupid little pouch thing rested on his hip. He stared at Jim from beneath the peak, a sneer in place.

Jim brushed past him, not wanting a confrontation about the noise last night. Not wanting anything but a bit of peace and quiet, somewhere to sort through the jumble in his head and contemplate the idea that someone was out to get them all.

He'd go where he usually did after Sunday dinner.

He turned left down the alley that would take him out onto a large expanse of grass and shrubbery by the main road. Massive stones had been placed there as seats, and he could take a pew and think for a bit, get things straight. He just had to hope no one was having a picnic, which wasn't unusual in the summer. The last thing he could cope with was squealing kids kicking footballs or zooming around on their bikes, their parents sunning themselves on red tartan blankets.

The alley was long and, lost in his thoughts, the whole world fading away, Jim got a jolt at coming out at the other end. Ahead, trees stood tall and proud, a small, thick copse that bordered the grassy area, leaves dense and abundant, summer's green clothes. Shouts from children filtered through, and he cringed. Maybe he could just sit with his back against a trunk and listen to the birds. Something, anything other than being at home.

He chose a trunk big enough to get his arms around if he fancied tree-hugging, which he didn't, and lowered to the ground. Spongy beneath his backside, it gave a bit of comfort, and he tipped his head back and shut his eyes.

For a second, he wallowed in the bliss, then Melinda and Keith did unspeakable things in his mind, Melinda smiling, doing that little gasp she always did when she—

No, he wasn't going to let this take over. Wasn't going to torment himself. Instead, he concentrated on the sound of his breathing and shut everything out, just *being*, glad to be alone. He drifted, sleep calling, and gladly succumbed.

* * *

David remained at the end of the alley, watching, waiting, his scuba helmet hiding his identity, the gloves bringing sweat to his palms. Seemed like Jim was going to sleep, and it wasn't any wonder. A party then staying up to talk to the police would make anyone tired.

To be honest, David hadn't expected Jim to carry on with his usual Sunday of visiting The Fox and Grapes. David going there on the off chance had been a good idea, because here they were, Jim nodding off, David ready to do the deed.

Jim and Melinda always came here after the pub, to walk off their dinner, he'd heard Jim say once. That this was going to happen earlier than planned was in David's favour. He'd nip into the pub for his own dinner. Alibi central.

He stifled a giggle.

Then, determination driving him to rid his lovely Casprey neighbours of the Le Huray bastards, he took the rope out of his bum bag and crept towards the tree. Jim was side-on, so David veered behind him, the sucking of oxygen loud in the helmet, and he hoped him treading on the springy ground wasn't creating too much noise. At the tree, he reached around to pass one end of the rope to his other hand, then, with it held tight, he lowered it level with Jim's neck.

And tugged it backwards.

Jim let out a hoarse sound of shock and lifted his hands to his throat. David held on tight, pulling, pulling, while Jim's legs flailed and his fingers scrabbled ineffectively at the rope.

The strength in David's arms weakened faster than he'd expected, and he gritted his teeth, pressing his boots to the base of the trunk for purchase. He leant back, letting his weight do the work for him. Something gave way — probably the hyoid breaking — and a slither of revulsion sprinted up David's spine. Jim's heels smacked a drumbeat on the copse floor, creating divots, and his arms flopped down. A look at one of his hands, palm up, revealed blood where Jim had fought to get the rope off. The stupid prat had probably gouged out his flesh.

Party Person was still now, but David continued yanking while casting his gaze about, anxious someone might come down the alley or a kid bounded in from the grass area. So he let go, dropping the rope, unwilling to ferry the evidence home with him this time. The sabre was different, it was something he wouldn't part with, and the food, well, he could take the rest of that to school tomorrow for his lunch.

He walked around to stand in front of Jim. Oh. What a sight. David hadn't thought about what they'd look like afterwards, and this one was a bit much. He strode away, unable to stomach such ugliness, waiting until he was three-quarters down the alley, then removed his helmet and gloves, stuffing them in the carrier bag he'd hung from his pocket, the baseball cap in the bottom. Next, he took off his black, long-sleeved T-shirt, the orange one beneath enough of a change to make him appear different to the man who'd leant on the pub window.

And noticeable to anyone watching.

Arms and hands aching, he strutted with purpose and entered the pub, exclaiming loudly to some old dear just inside the doorway that it was hot outside and his face must be red as anything.

He stood at the bar and ordered a lemonade and a beef roast with all the trimmings.

Killing was thirsty and hungry work.

* * *

Melinda stared out through her front window, tears streaming. They hadn't stopped all day so far, and they weren't because of Amanda or Dee. They were for herself, her predicament. She hadn't anticipated Jim catching her with Keith. In her mind, she'd played out the confession scenario over and over, where she told Jim the usual cliché that it was her, not him, and he should move on with someone better. In these daydreams, Jim begged, got down on his knees, crying his little heart out, and she always told him no, no, I can't stay with you. Then she'd make out she'd got together with Keith long after the breakup, and no one needed to know any different.

In reality, Jim had basically told her to fuck off, and *everyone* knew, and my God, it rankled. Things not going to plan always naffed her off. She'd messaged him earlier, several times, and he'd ignored her, as had Keith. And what was all *that* about? Keith was supposed to be in love with her, the bastard, and he usually responded to her straight away. Why not now? Didn't he want her when she was free? Or had she been a succession of quick shags in secret, a thrill, something taboo?

"Bloody knobrot," she muttered, thinking she should never have gone with Jim in the first place, but at the time, Keith had still been entranced by Amanda, and it had taken all Melinda's efforts to get him to see her in a light other than that of a friend.

The news of Amanda's death had been a relief, although Melinda had played the part of the grieving pal well, she reckoned. And as for Dee, she'd been watching Melinda and Keith like no one's business at every party lately, and she'd probably guessed what was going on. She must have been itching to tell Jim her suspicions, seeing as they were all buddy-buddy.

"Sod it."

She wiped her cheeks and told herself to sort this out, see where she stood. Bag grabbed, the handle slung over her shoulder, Melinda marched out of the house and over the road to Keith's. A policewoman stood outside Dee's, her attention on Melinda who was only going to see a bloody neighbour, nothing to write home about or get your knickers in a twist.

Not allowing herself to bear the indignity of knocking on his door and having him not answer, she went down the alley and opened the gate. In the garden, she glanced around. It was a state, and it would be. Melinda usually hung around to clean it up while Amanda and Keith lolled about on the sofa, and hadn't *that* been a mega cross to bear? It wasn't like she enjoyed housework. She'd only done it to breathe the same air as Keith for a bit longer.

The back door was locked and, grumbling about life being so difficult, she collected the key from beneath the flowerpot. It wouldn't go in the slot, though, so he must have left a key on the inside, the prat. Angry and on the verge of more tears, she strutted out, high heels clip-clopping, and tried Jim's next.

"He's at The Fox and Grapes," the copper called over.

How the hell did *she* know? What, was Jim seeing *her* now? Had he asked her out on the rebound? He didn't waste much time, did he. Incensed about that, she flounced past the woman, giving her the side-eye, and headed for the pub, wishing she'd put on her comfortable fancy trainers instead. It was too late now, so she pressed on, and by the time she got there, sweat had formed in all the places she hated, uncomfortable as eff.

She barged into the pub and looked around. Jim wasn't there. Maybe he'd nipped to the loo. Melinda approached the bar and asked the lady behind it if he was in. The negative answer upped her irritation, as did being told Jim had come in and then walked out again. What was he playing at?

Giving the place another once-over, and seeing no sign of Sarah or Bob either, she marched towards the door. Ugh, that horrible man who lived behind Keith sat there, scoffing a wedge of beef covered in gravy. He stared at her from his living room sometimes when she washed the dishes at Keith's, and she'd bet he didn't think she knew, the pervert.

Not giving him another thought, she rushed out onto the street, glancing left and right, unsure where to go next. Someone needed to be the brunt of her ire, and if she didn't find that person soon, she'd self-combust.

What if Jim was broken up about catching her with Keith and he'd gone to sit on the stones? Best she check, or she might lose her chance to blow her stack. She minced down the alley, turning her ankle and swearing loudly about it, getting out of breath and more incensed by the second. At the end, she stopped and stared.

"For fuck's sake, Jim."

What was he *doing* sitting there like that, his head bent to the side so only the top of it was on show? He had something red on his hand, like paint, and she wondered whether he'd finally decided to decorate his downstairs loo. The shade of Luscious Lips had sat for far too long in the corner beneath the little sink. He'd even taken to perching a pot plant on the tin. "Take's your eye off it," he'd said.

She grabbed at her hair in frustration, running towards him, her heels digging into the ground. God, they'd be ruined now, and it was all his fault. He could jolly well buy her a new pair.

She halted in front of him, glaring, her eyes hurting from the strain. What was wrong with him? Why did he have paint on his neck? Why was he gawping like a maniac and poking his tongue out? She kicked his leg, and he fell sideways, and still he stared.

It hit her then, what had happened, and she opened her mouth, letting out an almighty scream, her legs weakening. She crumpled to the ground, fumbling in her bag for her phone, and managed to unlock the screen. Who should she call? Which one would get here faster?

Someone came running from the picnic area, through the trees.

She accessed her contacts with a shaking finger and selected the name.

Then she screamed some more, irate that Jim had denied her the ability to rip him a new one, the selfish twat.

CHAPTER ELEVEN

"You *what*?" Bethany didn't think she'd heard right. "Say that again, will you?"

"Jim Ody is dead," Isabelle said, as though her mouth was too close to her phone.

"Tell me what happened." Bethany paced her office, the cheese and pickle sandwich sitting heavy, the taste of Branston thankfully killing that of the earlier bacon grease.

"Nicola said he went to The Fox and Grapes. Melinda went out afterwards. She found him in a copse down an alley by the pub."

"Why did *she* find him?"

"Apparently, she went to the pub to have a word, he wasn't there, so she thought he was at their usual spot, some stones or other."

"So how come you know? Why didn't Rob ring me like he usually does?"

"Because Melinda phoned Craig Gillan from the scene."

"Why him and not Keith?"

"Don't ask me. Anyway, I'm at the copse now."

"Who's with Dee?"

"She's still in situ. I called for another uniform. They sent Glen and a Tammy, not met her before. They were doing house-to-house, yes?"

"Yes. Tammy's new."

"Nice girl."

Bethany released a fat breath. "What a bloody mess."

"Well, Jim is."

"I don't want to know until we get there. Won't be long. Oh, and where's Melinda?"

"Still here. Thought you might want to question her straight away. There's also a woman with her. Got to go. The tent's going up."

"See you in a few. Shit, wait. What was that pub again?"

"The Fox and Grapes, three streets down from Le Huray."

"I know the one. Bye." She flew out of her office and into the incident room. "Jim Ody's copped it. Mike, let's get going."

Three shocked people stared at her, so she gave a brief explanation.

"This is looking more and more like the Obbington case," Leona said.

"I know. Three people dead inside twenty-four hours is a bit much. Someone is out of control if they haven't had a longer break in between." Bethany rubbed her forehead. "We need to go, so get your skates on."

She walked out and down to the car, gunning the engine at the same time Mike bounded into his seat. Screeching out of the car park, more from an energy rush than the need to get to the scene, she tried to sort through her cotton-wool mind. Was it Melinda? Had she killed Amanda because of Keith? Dee because . . . what? And Jim, that was an obvious reason.

"What the hell is going on?" she said. "This is screwing with my head. Melinda? Do you have her down for it?"

"What, Jim or the others?"

"All of them."

"With Amanda, it's possible. Melinda wasn't in the garden for quite some time. Dee? No way. Melinda lives opposite, so unless she can get across the street without being seen by Tory . . . And Jim, again, it's possible, but she'd have been spotted. Shit, I don't know. How was Jim killed?"

"No idea, but apparently he's a mess, according to Izzy."

"So a stabbing? I'm just guessing — don't answer. I don't even want to think about faces being grated off again. What else makes a mess?"

"Bludgeoning?" She wiggled a bit. "Christ, I forgot to have a wee before we left. This might not end well if I don't find a loo." Her bladder gave her a bit of gyp.

"That's what you get for rushing," he said, smiling.

"I'll nip in the pub — it's not like Jim is going anywhere, is it, and it won't hurt Melinda to wait an extra minute or two before we speak to her. There's also some woman with her."

"A woman? Go down that road there." Mike pointed ahead.

"Yep, so maybe she didn't do it if she has a friend with her." She rounded the corner and parked behind a SOCO van outside a house next to the pub.

They went inside, and Bethany headed straight to the toilets. Accident averted, she returned to the bar, where Mike questioned a server.

"So Jim came in and then left?" he asked.

"Yeah, he kind of stood and stared ahead, glanced to his right, seemed a bit spaced out, then buggered off." She swept a lock of hair away from her eye. "I was surprised to see him without Melinda, to be honest. Always in here on a Sunday, they are. And their mates, Sarah and Bob, they're not here either. Something going on, is it?"

"Do Bob and Sarah come in every Sunday as well then?" Mike tilted his head.

"Yep."

"How long after Jim came in did Melinda appear?" he probed.

"I don't know, maybe an hour? And she did the same thing. Came in, nosed about, asked if he'd been in, then went."

"Okay, thanks, you've been really helpful." He smiled at her and spun for the door.

"She looked like she'd been crying, that Melinda," she said.

Mike lifted a hand in a wave, and Bethany made for the exit. They ducked beneath police tape and walked down the alley. It was pretty long and Bethany scanned the ground for anything that seemed off. All appeared normal, but they'd better get a uniform down here to stand . . . Ah, Penny Dickens was at the end, so that saved Bethany the job of calling someone in.

She signed the log, suited up, then strode towards Melinda, who sat on the ground leaning against a tree to the left. The tent stood to the right. Someone must have cut a hole in it because a tree stuck out of it. But where was the other woman?

Melinda peered up, eyes soaked and red, a pink blush on each cheek, and scrambled to get up.

"Feel free to stay down there," Bethany said, glancing back at Mike.

He'd finished signing in, put on his white gear, and came over, getting his notebook and pen out.

"Tell me everything from the start," Bethany said.

Melinda did, her words tripping over themselves in her attempt to say everything so quickly. It seemed she'd wanted to have a go at Jim for whatever reason, so she'd come to the pub after Nicola had told her he was there.

"Why did you go to Keith's and then Jim's?" Bethany asked.

"I wanted to get some anger out."

"Why?"

"I'm so narked, you know?" She stuck her bottom lip out. "Neither of them answered my messages. It's not on."

Annoyance lifted the hairs on the back of Bethany's neck, and she thought of her own situation in her private life. "Don't you think grief might mean some people don't want to deal with their phones or people wanting their attention?" Bethany certainly hadn't wanted to entertain anyone else — still didn't. Mike had been the only one she'd let in from the start after Vinny had died. "Not everyone can bounce back straight away." *Like you.* A dig, but so what?

The woman was petulant, all about herself, and the fact her friends and ex-boyfriend were dead didn't seem to register or matter. Now Bethany looked back on it, Melinda hadn't been bothered last night either.

"I don't care," Melinda snapped, "they should have written back to me."

"Not everything is about you, love," Bethany said, the 'love' more sarcastic than kind. "So instead of giving Jim space, you followed him here."

Melinda rolled her eyes. "I didn't follow him, he'd already gone. When you follow someone, you're right behind them."

Bethany's irritation button had well and truly been pressed. "Listen to me, you. I'm not splitting hairs here, right? You went to the pub after Jim, saw he wasn't there, and left. You came here. Jim was . . . what? Tell me what you saw."

Melinda explained. Then, "And I thought it was his Luscious Lips paint, the one with the plant on top."

What the fucking hell is she on about? "Excuse me?"

Melinda elaborated, and Bethany had the very real urge to slap this bugging woman.

"Did anyone see you between leaving your house and entering the pub?" Bethany gritted her teeth.

"I don't know, do I!"

"Did you see anyone while on the way to the pub or here?"

"Can't remember."

"Well, you might bloody want to, because you need an alibi."

That shocked the little madam. Her face paled, and her mouth hung open.

"An alibi? What for?"

Bethany gestured to the tent. "You said yourself you were annoyed at Jim. You came here, and he's dead."

"It wasn't *me*!" She stumbled to her feet and planted her hands on her hips. "How can *I* kill someone? Look at me!" She held her arms out, showing off her slender figure. "See my hands? There's no way I've got rope burn. He's been *strangled*. That woman in the white suit told me."

Bloody hell. Must have been Isabelle. "Right, I'll arrange for someone to take you home. We'll need to speak to you again."

"Do you know what *I* need? A stiff drink. I'll be in the pub." She sauntered off.

"What you need is a lesson in humility," Bethany muttered.

"Blimey, imagine Jim and Keith being lumbered with that." Mike's forehead furrowed. "Her type is why I don't date these days. Too scared of ending up with someone like her."

"Isn't she just a delight? I doubt it was her, though. Not acting alone anyway."

"I thought the same. Strangulation. Tough job."

"Depends how it was done. She mentioned rope."

Isabelle popped her head out of the tent. "Ah, thought I heard you. The woman you need to speak to has gone back to her kids in the picnic area. You can't miss her. She has a turquoise top on and bright-blue hair, a bit like Marge Simpson."

"Thanks. We'll be with you in a minute," Bethany said. Then to Mike, "Who the hell is Marge Simpson?"

He laughed. "Cartoon character. We need to go there." He pointed behind the tent. "I can see people through the trees."

They walked that way, coming out onto a lovely setting — short-cut grass, large slabs of smooth, dark-grey stones, children playing. Blankets dotted the vicinity, food and drinks on top.

Bethany scanned for the woman. "Ah, there she is."

They approached her and produced their IDs.

"Hi, I'm DI Bethany Smith, and this is my partner, DS Mike Wilkins. I understand you were with a Melinda Nash in the copse there."

The woman nodded. "Well, not with her, but I ran to her when I heard her screaming." She arced a thumb over her shoulder at some children. "My kids are old enough to leave by themselves, so I didn't think twice but told them to stay put."

"Were you the only person who went to her out of all this lot?" Bethany indicated the surprising amount of activity. Folks had stayed here by choice with their little ones, when someone had been murdered and the killer could still be around? What was the world coming to?

"Yes." Marge-alike nodded again. "I suppose people are wary of helping these days. You don't know if you're going to get stabbed or something, do you? For a moment, I also wondered if the lady was screaming on purpose, to make people come running and then mug them."

"You have to be so careful, I agree. So, what did you do when you went into the copse?"

"I ran straight to her, didn't see him at first. You know, the bloke who'd been killed." She shuddered and wrapped her arms around herself. "She was screaming her head off, and I asked her what was wrong, whether she'd been attacked or whatever. She pointed at the tree, and that's when I saw the man. My legs went, know what I mean? But I think the mother in me came out, and I composed myself a bit, asked her if she'd called someone on the phone for help — she was holding her mobile — and she nodded and carried on screaming."

"What happened then?"

"I asked her if she'd killed him."

I bet that went down well. "And then?"

"She said, 'No, you stupid bitch, I found him like that.' I thought that was a bit rude, to be honest, but I put it down to her being frightened."

No, she's just a bitch.

Marge-alike went on, "So I got worried about whether some nutter was about. I left her so I could check on my kids, told another parent what had happened, and he said he'd watch my boys. Then I stood by the tree line where I could see her and my boys until the police arrived. I went back to her and chatted to a lady in a white suit. After that, I came here — the copper said it was okay so long as I waited for you."

"Did you touch anything?"

"No, not even her."

"Did you see anyone enter the copse from this side?"

"I didn't, sorry, but I *was* watching, because like you said, you can't be too careful."

"And are you okay?" *Stupid question?*

Marge shrugged. "It's not something I ever thought I'd see, no idea if I'll cope with it, but if I can go home now, that'd be great. I just want to get back to normality, if you see what I mean, plus get my kids away from here." She shivered, her blue hair wavering, a streak of it moving across to slap her opposite cheek.

"That's fine," Bethany said.

Mike took her name and address, and Bethany gave her a card with a list of therapists on it in case she felt she needed to see someone to talk about what she'd experienced, then they quickly questioned every other adult present. With no one seeing anything, they wandered back into the copse.

"I suppose we'd better get in that tent and see what happened to the poor sod," she said.

In they went, and Presley was there, too. He must have arrived while they'd been talking to Marge — his red car hadn't been out in the street by the pub.

Mike walked to stand in front of Jim. "Oh, sodding hell."

Bethany didn't move. Jim was on his side, the top of his head pointing towards her. Did she want to go and see the state of him? No, but she had to, so took a deep breath and stood beside Mike.

Sodding hell indeed.

A thick line marred his throat, reaching halfway round the sides, then nothing. His skin above and below it was bloodied and had been clawed, she assumed by Jim in an attempt to get the rope off. That rope, blonde in colour, sat over his legs, blood on a section of it where it must have dripped there from his self-inflicted neck wounds. His eyes had bulged and were wide open, as though he stared at them even after death, taking them in. The whites were red and the irises seemed to have lifted slightly, like an upside-down plate on a table. Cheeks, covered in a mass of petechiae, so much more than Dee's, created the illusion he'd been sunburnt, and his fingernails were thick with skin and blood. His hands too were streaked with the crimson stuff, and combined told a terrible story.

"Strangled from behind the tree," Presley said, "hence the rope burn not going all the way round his neck. The bark has been damaged, further supporting this theory. See how it's been rubbed either side?"

Bethany nodded. "It's at a level where Jim would have been sitting."

"Correct." Presley smiled. "I've already done the temp — he was killed up to an hour ago, possibly two, although he's cooling. It's shady in here, so it's not like we have the sun heating him."

How had Jim not heard someone coming? And if he had, had he remained seated because he'd known his killer and hadn't feared him or her? Or had he been standing and the killer subdued him, forcing him to sit against the tree?

"I don't know what to say," she said. "Three people killed in the space of a few hours. Whoever is doing this seems to want them gone quickly."

"Or they're killing them fast before they lose their courage," Mike said. "They might not want time to feel guilty."

She let out a weary laugh. "You think someone who can do this has the ability to feel guilty?" She shook her head. "This is either a highly unstable individual or an extremely angry one."

"Probably both," Isabelle said. "You can't tell me you're right in the head if you can think of so many methods of murder and act them out inside hours. A neck slice, a choking, a rope. If they're after everyone in Le Huray, which is obvious, what the hell are they going to come up with next?"

"I dread to think," Bethany said. "This person followed Jim, knew he'd be at the pub. It's got to be one of the people in the close, surely."

"The woman behind the bar said Sarah and Bob hadn't come in either." Mike folded his arms. "What if they're a tag team?"

It was something to think about, although the couple had seemed so nice.

"We'll have to go and speak to Craig, see if he knows why Melinda would pick him to ring, although she's already said Keith wasn't answering her," Bethany said. "And we still haven't been to see Vicky, Keith's ex. Let's do that now."

They left the tent, signed out of the log, and took their outer clothing off at the street end of the alley where a SOCO was on hands and knees scanning the path. In the car, she waited for Mike to join her, then set off.

What would Craig have to say? It might be a good idea to speak to Sarah and Bob too and ask them why they hadn't gone to the pub, although the obvious answer was that they were too upset.

"Another massive puzzle," she mumbled.

"Why expect anything less?" Mike said. "It's par for the course for us."

CHAPTER TWELVE

David stood behind the tall, thick hedge in his next-door neighbour's garden, which spanned the width of Jim's and Craig's, what with the houses in Casprey being bigger. Next door had gone off on holiday yesterday, so they wouldn't even know he'd stood here. Those in the first house in Casprey were also out, as usual, off to see the in-laws for Sunday lunch — roast chicken or minted lamb if they were lucky — and a nap, waking later for a bit of tea and cake. Victoria sponge, apparently, never anything different. They rarely returned before seven, and that suited David perfectly.

His beef roast had filled a hole, although he wasn't keen on the potatoes The Fox and Grapes served. They were the pre-roasted frozen kind, which always gave him indigestion. He worried he'd be a bit sluggish when sorting Craig out, but then again, what he had in mind didn't take much effort, although getting Craig to sit still might pose a problem. Maybe he'd have to whack him on the head with the hammer in his bum bag. Whatever, it'd be fun to see how this played out.

The scuba helmet's oxygen tank had been replaced for a new one — he couldn't risk it running out by bringing the other one he'd been using. He had five cannisters in all, so enough to see him to the end of his mission.

He stroked the helmet. The safety of anonymity fired his murderous blood.

Craig would be the second to last one for today. David had to have a bit of shuteye so he was ready to deal with the kids in school tomorrow. He was running on fumes, and offing Jim had taken more out of him than he'd thought it would.

He stared through the foliage at Craig's kitchen. The man himself sat at a small rectangular table, elbows resting on top, his head in his hands. He looked distraught, but that emotion wouldn't exist for him soon.

So there's that to be pleased about, Craig.

David silently laughed, his shoulders going up and down.

Craig lifted his head and cocked it, and David just made out a frown crinkling the man's forehead, his eyebrows beetled. Craig got up and walked through the double doors into the living room, veering to the left and out of sight.

Shit, had one of the others turned up to ruin it all?

Craig came back with the detectives. Had they found Jim? Earlier, David had thought about leaving his dinner and going after Melinda, but he had special plans for her and didn't want to deviate — although offing them both and posing them together would have upset Keith, which would have been nice. Never mind.

Craig sat at the kitchen table again, but the detectives remained standing. They talked for a couple of minutes and then left. Craig didn't get up to see them out. Instead, he walked to the back door and opened it, staring into the garden.

Could he see David? A thrill went through him at the thought, at the idea of Craig spotting a man all in black, the scuba helmet giving him a sinister appearance. It would freak anyone out. But Craig dipped his head and stared at his patio. As though he'd thought of something, he went back inside and through the kitchen to the lounge, where he stood behind the shield of the net curtains and gazed out into Le Huray.

David scrambled over the hedge, sticking a bit on top where some branches clutched at his long-sleeved T-shirt. Then he was in the garden, running, pausing at the flowerpot to get the key and pull his hammer out of his bum bag. He stepped inside and closed the door to. Crept through the kitchen, stopped at the double doors, and peered through the front window to see what held Craig's attention.

Jane Vanes was off out with her dog in the car. She did this every Sunday, taking the mutt to the forest a little way along from Shadwell Hill so he could 'have a good old run'. Jane usually arrived home around four, so that gave David plenty of time for the next one.

Craig seemed oblivious to his presence, the nosy bastard.

David carefully made his way towards him, raising the hammer. Just as he brought it down, Craig spun to face him, resulting in the hammer only catching one of the previously beetled eyebrows instead of embedding deep. It split the skin, and blood poured, some of it heading for the helmet.

Craig let out a scream and fell on his knees, clutching his head and rocking.

David dropped the hammer and grabbed Craig's biceps, hauling him across the room to plonk him in a chair. He took out his next 'weapon' and, while Craig was still disorientated and moaning, he wrapped the black cord around Craig's neck a few times, tight, leaving some to dangle like a skipping rope, the actual business end held in his gloved fist.

"I don't like your voice," David would have snarled if he'd been able to speak. He bent forward, hovering the bit that would kill over Craig's open mouth.

Craig must have registered that something was terribly wrong. His eyes widened, one covered in blood, the other slightly streaked with it, and he shook his head. "What . . . ? Who . . . ?"

It's me. The man who's going to end it all.

"What the fuck did you do that for? What do you want?" Craig raised a hand to tug at the cord.

You, dead.

He plunged the item into Craig's mouth, pushing it deep so the bulbous end wedged in his throat. Craig tried to launch himself out of the chair, but David was on him, straddling, digging his knees into Craig's lower ribs.

There, you bastard. How do you like that? Not going to sing for me now, are you?

David pinched Craig's nose, twisting it for good measure, bringing this crooning fucker more pain. While his victim made a valiant attempt at getting David off by pushing at his chest, David hummed *I Will Survive* in homage to this Party Person, closing his eyes to stop himself from seeing Craig's, which bulged, the whites turning red.

Sweat popped on David's face, and he sucked on the oxygen quicker, adrenaline pushing him to breathe faster. Or was that panic? So he didn't dwell on that, and now that Craig had gone still, he opened his eyes. Let go of his nose. God, his hand ached so much from that rope-pulling effort earlier.

Off Craig, he stood and stared until his breathing steadied and he drew in proper inhalations from the tank. Pleased this job had come to an end, he left the hammer where it was and exited the house, locking the back door behind him from outside, and popping the key on the glass-topped table under the kitchen window.

He scanned the Casprey houses.

No one at any windows.

With haste, he climbed over the hedge into his neighbour's garden, hid in the corner closest to his house, and took off the helmet, putting it in the carrier bag. Then he walked up the garden and took other keys from his pocket on a bunch. He entered the house, locked up, watered the indoor plants like he'd been asked to, put his gloves in his pocket, and strode out through the front.

Everyone in Casprey knew he kept an eye on this place whenever the inhabitants were away, so no eyelid would bat and no questions would be asked.

He ambled into his own place, washed the spurt of Craig's blood off the helmet, and put it in a clean bag. The weapon for the next job was at the victim's house, but what he *did* need from home he put in the bum bag, coiling it up tight, like a white, wicked snake, waiting to strike. Out the front again, he turned right and walked up the street, to the little track at the end. By the main road, he kept to the tree line beside it, shielded from view of any passing cars, the top end of the Casprey houses to his left. Then came Le Huray and where he'd killed Amanda. No police. No vehicles.

He darted down the sloping verge and into a small field behind Amanda's row, moving along close to the fences until he reached Lisa's. He put the gloves on. Checked the first-floor windows of Melinda's, Sarah and Bob's, and stared through a knothole in a wooden slat. Opened the back gate.

The stupid cow was in her garden, asleep on a sun lounger in an ochre bikini.

It couldn't have gone better.

David sidled past her and into the house through the open back door. Scanned the kitchen and unplugged what he needed. He took it with him upstairs and started a bath. While the water ran, he went into the spare bedroom and peered through the window at Lisa.

She was still asleep.

Good.

Once the bath had filled, he returned to the spare room, took the snake out of his bum bag and plugged it in — an extension lead. Then he plugged the thing he'd brought up from the kitchen into it. Checking the lead would reach the bathroom, and satisfied it did, he hid it all back in the spare room.

Beside the bath, he opened the window so Lisa would hear and swiped his arm across the sill so shampoo, deodorant, bubble bath, and all manner of things clattered to the floor, then legged it into the other room to hide, almost skidding on a pink disposable razor.

The sound of Lisa bombing it up the stairs was music to his ears, and again his breathing quickened.

"For fuck's sake!" she shouted.

He imagined her stepping into the bathroom.

"Bloody hell, Jane! Why run a bath and then piss off out? Not only do you do this, but my house stinks of those bloody scotch eggs you made."

Before she thought to pull the bath plug, he tugged the helmet on and was in there behind her. One shove to her back sent her sprawling forward into the water, and while she whacked her head on the far side, going under, and scrabbled in search of air, he grabbed the weapon and pushed down the lever. The inside lit up orange, and he rushed back into the bathroom.

Lisa sat in the water, knees up, arms around them, head bent, seeming to compose herself. Or maybe she was crying. Friends dying probably got you like that. Being pushed into a bath would, too.

Silent laugh.

She raised her face and stared at him, registering a male presence, eyes wide, mouth skewing into a suitable gaping hole perfect for screaming.

He threw the weapon — at her, on purpose, to ensure she reacted automatically. She caught it, but the momentum sent the object downwards, into the water, her still clutching it.

The electric current gripped her, holding her in its wicked embrace. She shot upwards from her muscles contracting, then sploshed back down, toes splayed, her hands resembling claws around the toaster, skin turning rapidly red.

She wouldn't be able to let go of that toaster if she tried.

That's for making breakfast for everyone, dragging out the parties.

He left, not wishing to see what else having a bath with an electric current did to a body, more intent on getting home and having a much-needed sleep. Out in the field, close to the fence, he took off his helmet and gloves, shoving them in the bag. The walk home was beautiful with him imagining her internal organs being damaged, the current careening through her, entering the heart and stopping it. She might well not die, just suffer, and while he preferred a clean sweep of death, her still living with a reduced quality of life was all right by him.

She wouldn't feel like partying ever again.

He glanced around.

No cars. No one out walking.

Marvellous.

Home called.

God, killing while deprived of sleep was taxing.

Still, his blue chair was waiting for him to sit in it and nod off, and that was all he cared about. Apart from killing the others. But tomorrow was another day.

* * *

David and Alan sat with Oliver York, the last kid on David's list of students who needed the 'we're here for you' talk. It had gone well so far, and those teens who had an iffy home life now knew they could come and talk to any teacher if they were overwhelmed. None of them had expressed the need to shoot up their fellow classmates, which had upset David a bit. He'd wanted to speak to someone of like mind, a person who had the same thoughts as he did.

"So what are you dealing with?" Alan asked Oliver.

"Mum's a bit of a druggy, innit." Oliver shrugged like he didn't care.

David would bet a pair of Nike Air that he did.

"That must be hard for you." Alan smiled sadly.

"Nah, I nick her drugs and sell them on." Oliver smirked.

"That's not a good path to go down," Alan said.

David always let his colleague deal with the questions for the most part. Safer that way. If he didn't blurt something out relating to how he felt, Alan couldn't suspect him later down the line when Dave started killing.

"It's what's on offer, though," Oliver said. "She's so off her face, she don't make dinner or buy me shit, like the stuff I need."

David studied Oliver. The lad had the latest clothing on, all brand names. Must have been bought with drug money.

"Does your mother know you steal her drugs?" Alan tapped something into his tablet.

"She just thinks she smoked more than she thought." Oliver laughed.

"Do you sell it to the children at school?" Alan frowned.

"Nope. They're all too goody-goody. I sell to blokes down the pub, innit."

"I'm going to have to ask you to stop doing that, Oliver." Alan paused. "Otherwise, we'll have to inform the police."

"I'll stop." Oliver didn't say it with any conviction.

"Good lad," Alan said. "Now, do you feel you need any support regarding your life? Someone to talk to?"

"We already have the social round, and they don't do nuffin."

Alan raised his eyebrows. "Nothing at all?"

"Nope. I'm fifteen. Another year, they won't have to care."

David couldn't resist stepping in here. "Does that make you angry?"

"It's all I've known."

"Do you have feelings of rage towards the system or your friends and schoolmates?"

"Nope. Not their fault they have good parents, is it?"

Bloody hell. This wasn't going how David wanted.

While Alan guffed on at Oliver, David thought about other options. He could talk to people online. People who wanted to chat about their urges to kill. No. That would leave a trail on his computer.

But what if he used one at school . . .

* * *

While his students were out doing cross country around the school field in preparation for sports day, David sat behind the door and logged on to one of the computers in the English department — those students were out practising their one hundred metre sprints.

He accessed Google, inputting words to search for what he wanted. The school boasted of trusting the kids, so parental controls hadn't been applied. David could wipe his search anyway, seeing as he was the IT teacher.

What he wanted seemed to twinkle out at him on page two, the third link down. He clicked and found himself in a forum, all the discussion topics on display. He opted for the one entitled EVER WANTED TO MURDER? *and had a good read.*

> *KillMartin2012: Ever get the urge to just stab the shit out of someone? [SEVEN KNIFE EMOJIS]*

> > *JoeBloggs: Not stab, no. Too messy.* ROFL.

> *KillMartin2012: JoeBloggs. Well, I want to stab this bloke called Martin. Seriously getting on my nerves. I work with him. He's a prick. I even think about killing him in my downtime. I mean, that isn't normal, is it?*

David itched to put his fingertips to the keyboard and reply to KillMartin2012. He couldn't risk it. Just reading ought to be enough, knowing someone else felt the same way he did. He glanced at the door at the sound of footsteps squeaking, held his breath, and then let it out when whoever it was had gone past.

> *JoeBloggs: I reckon everyone entertains killing at some point. Doesn't mean you have to act on it, though. Thinking about it doesn't hurt.*

> > *CherylBeauty: That depends, JoeBloggs. It can hurt* YOU. *If you keep thinking about it, getting annoyed at whoever's pissed you off, you end up full of anger, anxiety, and all the other stuff. Can't be good for you.*

> *JoeBloggs: Me? It's KillMartin2012 who wants to bloody kill someone. I just said thinking about it doesn't hurt.*

> > *CherylBeauty: I know you did, and the 'you' wasn't aimed at* YOU *specifically. Chill the fuck out, dickhead.*

> *JoeBloggs: CherylBeauty, who are you calling a dickhead?*

Bored by their spat, David scrolled farther down the discussion.

> *KillMartin2012: Well, I'm just saying. I have the proper need to kill Martin. Like, I have the knife and everything. I've worked out when to do it, too. He goes to the gym until late on a Saturday night. I'll get him then, in the car park out the back. No CCTV — already checked. He needs to be out of my life. Can't stay in my job if he's there. Tried to get him to leave, to get him in trouble so he's sacked, and it hasn't worked. I've been there longer than him, so why should I find a new job just because he can't behave himself?*

David smiled. At last. Someone who understood. It was a similar situation. Le Huray had been built after Casprey Lane. Everyone had been happy — peaceful — until that lot had moved in. The Party People needed to leave, not David. And they weren't likely to, so the alternative was to get rid of them.

Mind made up, David knew what he had to do.

He removed all evidence of his time on the computer, and then logged off. Out on the field, he cheered loudly at his class completing the final lap, acting as though he hadn't just been reading about the need to murder at all.

CHAPTER THIRTEEN

Jane called out to Yoda, her black-and-white collie. He came running, seeming to smile, dodging between trees, tongue lolling. She loved him so much, and if she hadn't been able to stay with Lisa while Felix, her husband, was away working, she reckoned the dog would be enough company to take the edge of loneliness away. You couldn't beat human interaction, though, and while Jane worked and spent time with her colleagues, it wasn't the same as sharing time with someone you loved.

While she threw a ball for Yoda, she thought about Lisa and her generosity. Jane didn't know what she'd do without her sister, to be honest, and even though Lisa had a snipe at her yesterday for boiling so many eggs, she was a good sort.

Maybe she should buy scotch eggs next weekend instead of making them herself. Mind you, would there even be another party this summer? The deaths had taken the happiness of such meetings away. How could they sit there laughing and getting drunk when people were dead?

Earlier, those officers in Dee's had come out, running to the van blocking the road and driving off as if something else had happened. It had given Jane the creeps.

Maybe I should move back home for a while.

She felt selfish for not including Lisa in that. When she got back, she'd tell her she was worried for their safety and they ought to get out of the close until the killer had been caught.

It was too dangerous to stay in Le Huray.

Jane had asked Lisa to come with her on the walk today, so they were together, but Lisa had wanted to sunbathe. Not even the idea of the shade from the trees here had persuaded her, so she must want to get a base tan for when she went to Antigua with Melinda. Felix would be back for two months then, so Jane and Yoda would go home.

Yoda bounded over and dropped the yellow ball at her feet. Despite her grief, she couldn't help but laugh at him staring up at her, waiting expectantly, tail wagging. She threw it again, up the track, and remembered the bodies that had been found here in the spring. Quickening her step past the burial sites, now hidden by the abundance of foliage on the forest floor, she shoved murder out of her mind and tried to think of nicer things.

And failed.

"Come on," she called to the dog, scared here with no other walkers about. "Let's go back."

It was earlier than her usual return time, but she had an uneasy sensation she ought to be with Lisa. In the garden, Lisa was vulnerable, especially with that open field out the back, and with Amanda being left in that area . . .

She turned and jogged down the track, Yoda scampering after her, soon overtaking. He waited for her beside her car, and she reached him, out of breath. He jumped into the back seat, and she drove to Lisa's faster than usual, her sense of something being wrong growing. Maybe it was just the murders that had her feeling this way, but whatever it was, she wanted to pack their bags and go and stay at hers instead.

Parking in Lisa's drive, she let the dog out and entered the house. Yoda scrabbled on the hallway laminate, then the kitchen floor tiles, as usual, unable to gain purchase on the shiny surfaces. He pinged out into the garden, sniffing at all the bushes on his way to the bottom, cocking his leg while he was at it.

Lisa wasn't out there.

Jane made to leave the kitchen, but something was off. What was it? A burning smell? She stared at the worktop in front of her. A rectangle of crumbs sat where the toaster usually was. Why had Lisa moved it? And where to?

Frowning, Jane couldn't see it so went into the lounge at the front. No Lisa. At the bottom of the stairs, she got the God-awful idea that Lisa was hurt, and that burning smell was stronger. Guts cramping, she called out to her, gripping the newel post as if it would give her strength and stop her from feeling this way.

It didn't.

"Lisa?"

With no answer, she climbed the stairs and, halfway up, frowned again, stopping short. Why was there a bloody extension lead going from the spare room into the bathroom? Surely Lisa wasn't stupid enough to plug a radio or phone in. They'd had a discussion about this before, and until Lisa's phone contract was up and she could make sure she had a new waterproof one, there was to be no phone, charging or otherwise, while she took a bath. Had she reneged on her promise, because Jane had gone out and wouldn't have known any different if she'd stayed in the forest until her usual time?

Imagining Lisa dead in the bath from a phone electrocution, she continued up. More signs of worry caught her attention — all the things from the windowsill were on the floor.

She rushed in, heart thrumming, her legs going weak, and stared at the bath.

An immediate need to vomit swept over her, but her knees buckled, and she flopped to the floor, screaming so hard her throat hurt.

* * *

"Who the hell was that?" Sarah said to Bob over the roof of their car, shoving the last suitcase on the back seat so they could get away from here and go and stay with their son for a while.

They stared at each other in shock for a moment, then Bob was off, haring across their front garden and down the far side of the house. Sarah followed, trailing him out to the field. Bob turned right at the bottom of the fence, and she was hot on his heels, catching sight of him disappearing through the gate into Lisa's back garden. She went in, too, expecting him to be getting the key out from under the flowerpot, but the back door was open, and Bob was nowhere in sight. Yoda pranced about on the patio.

The scream had shut off abruptly when they'd been out the front, but what if that was because Lisa or Jane were dead? What if Jane was the killer? She'd not long arrived back from taking Yoda out — Sarah had seen her through her living room window — and . . . and . . .

"Fucking hell," she muttered, entering the house. "Bob? Are you okay?"

Images of him being killed next sauntered through her mind — that would teach her for reading so many scary books. To her, a shoe on the side of the road meant someone had been abducted, and a black bag of rubbish always had a body inside it in crime thrillers. Her mind leapt to these conclusions on a daily basis, and now people were being killed left and right, it was understandable to be worried.

"Up here," Bob shouted. "Go out and get that copper."

"But she wasn't there when we were putting the cases in the car. What's happened?"

"Just ring them then, call an ambulance as well, but get out of here," he said.

She opened the front door and went outside, scanning the street. The policewoman was there now, thank God.

Sarah darted across to her. "Something's happened in there, I don't know what."

The copper grabbed her radio and spoke into it as she sped across the close, then called back, "Stay there!"

Frightened to death, Sarah did as she was told, shaking, her skin going cold despite the heat of the afternoon. Was the killer watching her? Hiding somewhere?

A uniformed policeman came from behind her, scaring her silly, and stopped by her side.

"Oh shit, shit!" she said, hand on her heart.

"Are you all right?" he asked. "Sorry if I frightened you."

She nodded, even though she *wasn't* all right. How could she be after this?

"I'm Glen," he said.

"Hello, Glen." Why did she say that? This wasn't some pleasant bloody meeting, for God's sake!

"Would you prefer a woman to stand with you? My colleague is inside Dee's."

Sarah nodded again, teeth chattering, and he spoke into his mobile. A young lady in uniform came out, and Glen went back into Dee's. Sarah wondered if they had to keep watch over the body or something. Where had the first policewoman gone earlier? For a wee? Or to kill Lisa and Jane — that could happen, couldn't it, a copper going rogue? God, this was all so horrible, and it sounded mean, but if they'd been a few seconds quicker, they'd have been in the car and on their way, none the wiser.

You mustn't think like that . . .

But it was a natural thought. Self-preservation.

The policewoman smiled and touched Sarah's arm. She jumped, nervy, wondering what the hell Bob was going through at Lisa's. What had he found? He'd said about an ambulance. That meant Lisa and Jane were alive. She nearly sagged to the ground with relief.

"I'm Tammy Hill. Can you tell me what happened?"

"An ambulance," she said. "Bob said to ring one . . ."

"It's fine, that'll be dealt with now." Tammy guided her to the side of Dee's. "Are you ready to talk about it?"

Sarah went through what she knew while Tammy wrote notes. It was surreal. The words came out of Sarah's mouth, matching the images in her head as she saw it all over again, but it was like she viewed things from deep inside herself, where she hid from the terror and peered through eyes that weren't her own, as if autopilot was taking over and getting her through this.

She stared ahead at Lisa's open door, registering Bob coming out with Jane beside him, glimpsing them through a tunnel, blackness in her peripheral.

"Oh God," she said, cutting her story off, wanting to go over there and see to Bob, and to make sure he was okay.

"Stay with me," Tammy said.

Sarah must have moved to run across the road or something — Tammy held her wrist, not tight, but enough to keep Sarah from going any farther. Bob guided Jane towards them and gently pushed her shoulders so she lowered onto the grass. Sarah stared, all sense gone from her, as though she needed someone to tell her what to do in order to function. Then Tammy was dealing with Jane, and Bob had his arms around Sarah. She cried with happiness that he wasn't hurt.

"What happened?" she asked, her real self coming back to her, slowly but surely. She looked up at him. His ashen face hurt her soul.

He shook his head. "You don't want to know. Not yet." To Tammy, "We'll be at home. Number eight."

"Make sure you stay there, please, until someone's spoken to you," Tammy said.

He helped Sarah home much as he'd helped Jane outside, and she'd never been so pleased to have her husband with her in her life. In their living room, they stood at the window and gazed out.

"Lisa?" she asked.

"Gone, love."

Chills rippled through her, and she clutched his hand, holding on tight. "We need to leave. As soon as the police have talked to us."

"We need to leave full stop," he said. "Someone's out to kill us all."

She whipped her head round to stare at him. "What?"

"That policeman told me that's what they think."

"P-p-pardon?" Once again, she retreated inside herself. She was giddy and all she could see was her Venetian blinds rocking from side to side, knowing they actually weren't. "Oh . . ."

"On the sofa, darling, that's it."

She sat, her heart hurting from how hard it beat, her whole body seeming hollow. "What's happening?"

Then the tears came. Tears of horror, bewilderment, sorrow, of living in a street where someone was out there, waiting to murder them, too. "Oh God, we left the front door open when we went to Lisa's. What if someone's upstairs?"

He moved to the front door. "The ambulance is here. Let's go outside."

She didn't want to see Jane carted off or at the very least being tended to, but it was better than being inside where a killer might be lurking. That got her off the sofa and out into the warm air, Bob right there with her.

Melinda sauntered into the close, staring with her mouth open. "What the fuck's going on *now*?"

It came out as a shriek, and Sarah winced.

Melinda tottered over, clearly the worse for drink, and she didn't smell nice, like she'd sprayed wine all over herself.

"Jane's hurt?" she asked.

Bob nodded. "And Lisa's dead."

"You're having a laugh," Melinda said.

"You'd be better off doing what we are once we've been interviewed," Bob said.

"And that is?" Melinda always had been a snippy cow. Why had Lisa even wanted to go on holiday with her?

"Drive away," Bob said. "And never come back."

CHAPTER FOURTEEN

"It was a good job Vicky Trannor didn't have much to say and we were almost at the end of questioning her." Bethany sped towards the Warburg estate, blue lights flashing.

Glen had phoned her to relate what had happened, and Mike had rung Isabelle as soon as they'd got in the car. Her shriek had sailed out of the phone and assaulted Bethany in the driver's seat. Then he'd let Fran and Leona know the latest.

As for Vicky, she'd said Keith was a player and a dickhead who had messed her about when he was supposed to have their son, but he wasn't a killer. Her reaction to him seeing Melinda behind Amanda's back hadn't been a shock, but she'd appeared saddened on Amanda's behalf.

"And isn't that just weird?" she'd said. "She took my husband from me, and now I've got sympathy for *her*!"

"Probably because you know how she'd have felt if she'd found out about them," Bethany had said. "But there is a lady called karma who delivers these kinds of presents when she can manage it, and had Amanda still been alive, she'd have experienced what you did at some point."

While Vicky might not think Keith a murderer, at one time, she said she hadn't thought he'd cheat either, so . . . *Could it be him?*

Frustrated, Bethany said, "What the bloody hell is going on here?"

"Do you even want me to answer that?" Mike rested his elbow on the open window frame, the breeze from the car's movement ruffling his shirt sleeve. "Because it'll be me stating the obvious."

"What, that everyone in Le Huray is a target?"

"Yep."

"Fair point."

She shuffled through her mind what was currently being done. House-to-house had brought up nothing in the surrounding areas, although Fran and Leona were currently checking alibis for those who didn't have neighbours to back them up, like folks out having Sunday pub dinners, being at a family home elsewhere, or shopping and the like. A couple of the extra uniforms were en route to Casprey Lane to determine whether anyone there had seen or heard anything regarding the latest death in Le Huray.

"So it's Lisa dead this time," she said. "Why not Jane, too, when they live together?"

"We'll find out when we get there."

She parked up behind the SOCO van at the entrance to Le Huray. It was a different one to before — the number plate wasn't the same — so Isabelle must have called in her third team and left the second one at the copse. The first would be at home, sleeping the day away having worked on Amanda's site.

Out on the path, she tried the SOCO van door, and it opened. Finding protective clothing, she handed a set to Mike, and they set off across the street to number six, where Tammy stood at the front door holding a log.

"Bet you didn't expect this when you offered to do overtime," Bethany said to her, signing in then getting her overalls on.

"No, and this is much more than I thought I'd be involved in." Tammy handed the log to Mike. "Bicester had nothing as severe as this."

Bethany zipped up her suit. "Well, we've had a lot of murders taking place round here lately, so brace yourself for this sort of thing in the future."

Mike was nearly dressed. "What with Shadwell and the next town over, we're going to hit the list as the worst locations for murder in the UK at this rate. Maybe it's something in the water." He stuck a hat on.

Bethany did the same and tucked her hair away. "Well, with unemployment here at an all-time low and jobs being scarce, it's no wonder people are down, and that can lead to discord. Don't get me wrong, that isn't an excuse for these killers, but a person's surroundings and situation can affect their outlook, and sometimes, all it takes is one small thing to set someone off. Anyway, that's a lesson for another day." She smiled.

"You might want to study up on that. It's fascinating," Mike said to Tammy. "Watch a few documentaries, that'll set you right. You've got to understand how they work in order to deal with them — the criminals, I mean."

"I will," Tammy said. "Thanks."

Bethany and Mike entered the house, and Bethany pushed the door so it almost closed.

"I like her," she said quietly. "She'll go far."

"You'll be nabbing her for the team before long."

"How did you know?"

"Because you haven't taken that much interest in the other uniforms."

Bethany laughed. "She's got four years under her belt as a plod, and she'd need to spend twenty weeks in training and two years' probation for a DC. Providing she passes the exams required, she could officially be with us after that, and she'd be useful out on the streets like us. There are times when Fran and Leona are strapped with office-based work and can't always get out in the field. Anyway, we need to park this convo and see what the chuff's happened to Lisa."

"Up here," Isabelle called.

Bethany bypassed a SOCO on the stairs, who stared at a riser as if it were the most interesting thing he'd seen all day. At the top, she looked ahead at Isabelle in the bathroom.

"Photos have been taken," Isabelle said, "so don't worry about stepping around the mess on the floor. Besides, Jane's muffed that right up. She came in and disturbed the evidence."

Several beauty products littered the small space.

"And enter one at a time," Isabelle continued. "It's very cramped with more than three people." She glanced at a SOCO dusting the windowsill. "Good job Lisa's in the bath really." She sighed. "Actually, I'm going to step out while you have a gander."

Bethany cringed. With that singed extension lead snaking into the bathroom, plus the smell, she didn't need to wonder what had happened.

Isabelle came out. "Don't worry, the power shorted, and it's been switched off in all areas of the house."

Bethany tentatively stepped in. "Shit . . ."

Lisa's legs were straight out in front of her, toes spread. The skin had burst in places, the yellow of fat globules and red muscles peeking through. She'd sunk beneath the water clutching a toaster — *What the fuck?* — her hands and arms burnt, black and charred as if left on a barbecue for too long. She could have killed herself quite easily, but with other Le Huray residents dead, it wasn't likely.

Bethany didn't look at her face. She knew what the poor woman was likely to resemble, and it wasn't pretty, so she focused on her clothing instead. Lisa's bikini, had she committed suicide, could have been to preserve her modesty, her not wanting whoever found her to see her private parts, but with a murder, it was indicative she'd perhaps put it on due to the weather being hot or had planned to go swimming, putting her clothes on over the top to save time at the pool.

Having seen enough, Bethany left the room, and Mike went in. His muttering "Fuck me sideways . . ." wasn't surprising.

He joined them on the landing, paling. "That is *nasty*."

"A toaster, though . . ." Isabelle shuddered.

Bethany shook her head. "I'm not going to hang around up here. It's too much. I'll go and find Glen to get the details of what went on. He didn't say a lot on the phone, just that she was dead and we needed to get here quickly."

"Will you be speaking to Presley?" Isabelle asked.

"Yes, but I'm not going back into that bathroom. See you in a bit." Bethany went downstairs and spoke to all the SOCOs in turn to see if they'd found anything. Negative answers given, she met Mike on the doorstep.

"So if you put in to be a DC," he was saying to Tammy. "Ah, here's Beth. I was just telling Tammy about the opportunities available here."

Bethany smiled at the uniform. "What do you think, Miss T?"

Tammy nodded. "Mike says it's twenty weeks of training, then probation. Do you think I'd be allowed to do that on your team?"

"I doubt Kribbs will have a problem with it. The chief isn't a scary sort, and if I tell him I need more help, especially with cases like this . . ."

"Okay, I'll look into it. Thanks!" Tammy smiled.

"Let me know when you decide so I can put the wheels in motion on my end," Bethany said. "Now, where's Glen?"

"He's next door in number seven with Jane, Sarah and Bob," Tammy said.

"Thanks."

Bethany walked to that front door then went inside. Mike followed, and she found them all in the lounge. Sarah had been crying, going by the state of her face, and sat by Bob on the sofa, his arm around her. Jane curled up on a chair, a dog on her lap hugging her, his paws on her shoulders. Glen stood beside the doorway. Bethany jerked her head at him, and Mike took his place while Bethany and Glen moved outside.

"What happened?" she asked, closing the front door a bit.

"I bloody hate saying this, but Nicola left her spot outside Dee's to get a quick drink of water. As you know, Tory was at Dee's back door. She told her to get back out the front. In the time Nicola was gone, Sarah and Bob had been putting suitcases in the back of their car — they were going to stay with one of their sons for a while. Prior to this, Jane was at the forest to take the dog for a run. Lisa was sunbathing. Jane came home. Nicola saw her arrival, plus Sarah and Bob putting the first lot of cases in their car, then she went for that drink. Sarah and Bob heard a scream so ran round the back to get into Lisa's — they'd planned to use the key under the flowerpot. The back door was open, though, so Bob went in and found Lisa in the bath and Jane screaming on the floor. He didn't check Lisa for a pulse — not with that toaster in the water and Lisa being submerged — and instead asked Jane what was going on. She'd come home, couldn't find Lisa, then searched the house."

"How long was Jane out with the dog?"

"Just over an hour."

"Then what happened?"

"Well, while all this was happening, Nicola was back at her post. Sarah came out of the house saying help was needed. Nicola called in the issue on the radio and entered Lisa's."

By the time he'd finished telling her the rest, also saying SOCO were out the back of Lisa's checking the field behind the houses for any clues, Bethany was between two emotions: anger towards Nicola but at the same time feeling sorry for her. Why hadn't she phoned Glen or Tammy to stand at her post? The pair of them had been inside Dee's. In a split second, a killer had possibly walked into the street and straight to Lisa's unobserved.

"Christ," she said.

"But this could be saved," he said, kicking at a loose stone on the path.

"Meaning?" Was he implying what she thought he was? And how did she feel about that? *I don't know.*

"You chew Nicola's arse but not mention it to anyone else. You know, what she did." He blushed. "Sorry, that was below the belt. I just don't want Nicola to get hauled over the coals. It was a lapse in judgement. The close was so quiet . . ."

"A fucking big lapse when murder is involved."

"Well, that's just it. A SOCO was in Dee's front bedroom and noticed Nicola walk away, so he stopped dusting the sill and kept watch while she was gone. No one entered the street."

Relief ploughed into Bethany. "Right. Right. Um . . ." How should she play this? "Has Bob and Sarah mentioned Nicola being gone?"

"Yes."

"Then it can't be swept under the rug. If Nicola ends up in the doghouse, she'll just have to deal with it. Harsh, I know, but with someone being killed . . ." An idea occurred to Bethany. What if Sarah and Bob just hadn't seen Nicola from their position? Their house or Melinda's at number eight weren't opposite Dee's, they were farther along, level with Craig's and Jim's. *This could work* . . . "Okay, leave it with me."

"What about my paperwork?" he asked. "What do I say?"

This was where slippery slopes came into it. Was Bethany prepared to go skidding down one if she allowed her fellow officers to lie to save one of them getting into trouble? If she lied herself? "Fuck it. Come with me."

She led him over the road to where Nicola stood.

"Go and get Tory a second," Bethany ordered her.

Nicola, red-faced and clearly scared, did as she'd been told. Bethany and Glen stood in silence, waiting. When Tory and Nicola appeared, Bethany tapped Glen's elbow and led him to halfway down the side of Dee's house to meet up with them.

"Is Nicola in the shit?" Tory whispered.

"Do you want her to be?" Bethany stared at her. She had to gauge whether Tory was willing to go all in on this with them.

"Of course not. I know it isn't right, and I'm not a bent copper, but is there some way we could . . . ?" Tory's cheeks flushed.

"Then we're all on the same page." Bethany took a deep breath. She could get herself in a mess with this, but these uniforms . . . she cared about them. They worked together a lot. *Just say it.* "I do *not* want this going any further than us lot and Mike. If what occurred gets out, I'm denying all knowledge of it, do you understand?"

The three nodded.

"Then this is what happened," Bethany said. "Listen to me and get it straight in your heads. Nicola" — she pointed at her — "you moved to stand beside Dee's house but could still see the whole close. You only took one step back from the front outer wall. Tory, you didn't see her come in for a drink, end of. Glen, you know nothing except you were called out by Nicola when Jane screamed. Nicola, you could see Sarah and Bob putting a second set of cases in their car just before the scream, got it?"

More nods.

"Your statement will reflect that, right?" Bethany raised her eyebrows at Nicola, who cried.

Tory smiled. Glen let out a sigh of relief.

"Nicola, you're just lucky a SOCO was looking out onto the street and saw no one enter," Bethany said, "otherwise, you'd be fucked. Now, this goes against protocol, we all know that, and I *do not* expect to be called into Kribbs' office over this. Am I clear?"

"Oh God, thank you." Nicola wiped her cheeks.

Bethany allowed them a small smile. "Get back to work — don't let me regret this. I'll arrange for you three and Tammy to be relieved, because you've all been working stupidly long hours."

She turned and walked back to Sarah's, Glen behind her.

What have I done?

* * *

After interviewing Jane, Sarah and Bob, as well as taking the married couple's son's address so she could contact them while they were staying there, she stood in the close with Mike, telling him about the Nicola situation.

"Are you in?" she asked. "I understand if you'd rather not be a party to it."

"Of course I'm in," he said, "although Nicola is a silly bloody cow for doing what she did."

"I know. Bet she doesn't repeat that again. But she's been working for hours. It's hot. It would only take a second to get a drink. You can see her thought process."

"All the same . . ."

"Moving on . . . We need to speak to the remaining residents and see if they saw or heard anything. I noticed none of them are out in the street or over with Jane giving her a shoulder to cry on apart from Sarah and Bob. Her sister is dead, for Pete's sake."

"Hmm. Craig first?" he asked. "I can't cope with Melinda right now."

"Glen said she came back from the pub earlier and has gone home. We'll need to verify she was there. Fucking hell, I'm starving. It's got to be close to dinner."

"Take a break after this? Eat at The Fox and Grapes while we're there and questioning them about Melinda?" Mike looked hopeful.

"Yep. Come on." She trudged over the road, so weary, calling into the station on the way to get the uniforms relieved.

Mike knocked on Craig's door. They waited for a few seconds, then he rapped again. Impatient, Bethany stepped onto the grass below the living room window and peered inside. The nets were the voile kind, and she couldn't get a clear view this close.

"We'll go round the back," she said. "Maybe he's in his garden."

Down the path between Craig's and Dee's, Bethany rounded the corner. Craig wasn't outside, but a key sat on a glass table. Still with her protective clothing on, she reached out and picked it up, the gloves sticking to her skin from sweat. She gained entry and stepped inside.

"Craig? It's DI Bethany Smith." Moving farther into the kitchen, she stared through into the living room. "Oh, for crying out loud!"

Mike brushed past her and dashed to Craig, pressing his fingers to the man's wrist. He turned to Bethany and shook his head. "This is insane."

"You could call it that."

Craig had been struck on the eyebrow, and blood covered half his face, spatter on the other. A black lead was around his neck, and a microphone stuck out of his mouth.

"If these deaths aren't tailored to the victims, I'll eat my fucking hat," she said.

"If you had a hat."

"Shut your face."

Craig had sung karaoke at the party. Now they just had to work out what the blade meant for Amanda, the food for Dee, the rope for Jim and the toaster for Lisa. Knowledge the killer knew.

"Sarah and Bob are going to be all right with their son," she said, "but Melinda, Jane, and Keith are going to need to go elsewhere for now. It isn't safe for them to live here at the moment. Should we have done that before now? Were we wrong to let them stay here?"

"It's all happened so quickly." Mike walked over to her. "We didn't expect the killer to work so fast."

"Whoever it was must have got in round the back of Lisa's and here." She closed her eyes for a moment. "Keith. He could have gone up the alley beside his house, into Casprey Lane, and walked along the main road to get to Lisa's."

"With SOCOs in Jim's garden?"

"Hmm, didn't think of that."

"Go to Keith's next?" he asked.

She nodded. "Let me just give Isabelle a ring. She's going to have a shit fit."

CHAPTER FIFTEEN

David woke from a lovely nap. A bottle of tonic water stood on the table beside the blue chair, and he took a healthy swig. He stared out at Keith's then stood, peeking over at Craig's.

Oh. Movement.

White. Police in those outfits.

So they'd found him then. Not surprising with the number of coppers swarming the area. Had they found Lisa, too? Shame he couldn't get a clear view down the gap between Keith's and Jim's. He could have worked out whether they'd discovered her by the activity in the close.

He looked at the clock. It was past four, when Jane usually returned with her dog. Safe to say Lisa's death was known. He imagined Jane screaming. What a pity he hadn't been awake to hear it through the open window. He reckoned it would have travelled that far.

He had the urge to walk down the alley beside his and Keith's. Peer round into Le Huray and see what was going on, but that would be disastrous. Putting himself in the limelight. Some killers did that.

Loud laughter. Head thrown back.

The police had their hands full, so he'd give them some respite.

Tomorrow, though, was another matter.

More laughter.

* * *

"Hey, fans," Keith said, strutting out of his house into the garden, hands outstretched like he was bloody famous, the twazzock.

David, in his usual place by the hedge, gritted his teeth. Fans. Keith really thought his neighbours saw him as the star of the show, just because he hosted the parties? He was always saying it, implying they were his groupies. Who did he think he was?

The man got right on his wick.

"What about a game of spin the bottle?" Keith suggested.

His wife, Vicky, gave him a filthy look. "Um, excuse me? Really not appropriate."

"Who said you had to play?" Keith stared at her with that stupid smirk of his.

Vicky got up. "I think I hear your son waking up anyway. Someone has to be a decent parent and spouse around here." She flounced off inside.

The sound of Keith's "Whoo, get you, stroppy pants!" followed her.

What a despicable man.

David wanted to vault the hedge and smack Keith's head in. He clenched his fists, the noise of him sucking in oxygen filling the helmet, white noise, and rage building inside him. These people really did have to go. None of them had gone after Vicky. Instead, they'd remained silent in their garden chairs, sipping drinks, picking at the sandwiches Dee had brought out earlier. Dee herself had a plate full of food. The sandwiches. Cocktail sausages. She bit into a scotch egg.

I wish you'd fucking choke on that.

"Right, who's up for it?" Keith said, clearing one of the tables and laying an empty wine bottle down on his side.

He spun it. The open end pointed at Amanda.

"A kiss," he said, grabbing her hands and pulling her upright.

She didn't seem to have any qualms about locking lips with him.

David glanced up at the bedroom window.

Vicky looked down.

Oh dear.

Everyone erupted in a chorus of jeers and shrieks of either shock or surprise.

"Keith! What the hell?" Melinda said.

Ah, she wasn't best pleased. She'd been panting after Keith for a long while now. Dirty bitch. David hated the way she showed off her tits, flaunting herself.

"Keep the noise down, will you?" a female neighbour from Casprey shouted. Was that Elaine?

"Fuck off," Lisa yelled.

"That fella out the back is going to phone the police again," Craig said. "You mark my words."

"Ah, give him enough rope and he'll hang himself." Jim shrugged. "The police will have him for wasting their time, keep ringing them like he does."

No, he won't. *David thought of his plan.* I'll use the rope on you.

CHAPTER SIXTEEN

Glad to be out of protective clothing for a bit, Bethany asked Keith, "So you've been home all day?"

He slumped in a chair, legs open, his shorts a bit baggy, giving a view of something she'd rather not have seen. He didn't have boxers on.

I'm hungry, but that kind of meat and two veg is a bit much.

"Yeah. I got woken up earlier by some of you lot," he moaned. "They wanted to do their thing in my bedroom." He raised his shoulders. "Fine by me. Got nothing to hide. They were here ages, so if you think I could get out without them or that copper on the corner seeing me, you're a bit dim."

So SOCO had returned to finish going over his house. She was glad he didn't seem bothered by it. But was he pretending? Making out he was okay with having his house poked through while he'd slept, then again later on?

"As you'll understand, with Amanda's death . . ." She smiled tightly.

"Yeah, yeah, you have a job to do. And you know I was still here when Dee got . . . and Jim. If you think it's me, you're barking up the wrong bloody tree."

"What did you do after SOCO left?"

"Made a bit of lunch — a late one, granted. Played COD."

"The game?"

"Yeah."

"Online or off?"

"Online. There's a group of us that get together on Sunday afternoons."

"Friends of yours?"

"Not in real life, no. I just know them from the game."

If they had to, they'd take his Xbox and check the time Keith had been playing, but although she'd suspected him from the start, his manner, how laid back he was, now . . .

"How do you feel about your neighbours being killed?" she asked.

He shrugged again. "What do you think? I'm gutted."

He didn't look it, but maybe he was the type to hide his emotions. Stick his head under a rock by playing COD and pretending everything was all right.

"Craig and Lisa have also been murdered." She held her breath for a reaction.

He sat forward, slowly, and rubbed his chin. "Seriously?"

Well, it's not something I'd pissing joke about, is it.

She studied him. It was as if he had to take time to process, the information too much to handle. He frowned. Shook his head.

"When? How?" He stared her straight in the eye.

"Earlier today. Craig had a microphone jammed in his throat, and Lisa was electrocuted in the bath by a toaster."

"Eh?" His forehead lines grew deeper.

"Do you know why a toaster would have been used?" With the manner of Craig's death linked to singing, she was desperate to understand Lisa's.

"A toaster . . ." Monotone.

"We think each death has been tailored to the person." Mike, maybe stepping in to see if Keith responded better to a man. "Imagine your friends. What does the method say to you regarding them?"

"I don't know!" Keith said, exasperation drenching his tone.

"Then think!" Mike snapped. "You could be next, for God's sake."

Keith moved forward, to the edge of the chair, and dug his elbows into his knees. He lowered his head in his hands. "This is just stupid, what I'm thinking, but . . ."

"Whatever your thoughts are, tell us," Bethany urged. "Something that may seem silly and insignificant to you might be extremely significant to us." Or the killer. Some had the strangest reasons to commit murder.

Keith sighed. Stared at the floor. Gripped his head harder. "Amanda. The knife. I remember someone saying once at a party she was cutthroat in how she went after me. How she flirted then let me kiss her at one of the parties, even though Vicky could walk out into the garden at any second. I was unhappy in my marriage; it was my choice to cheat. I engineered it so we kissed the first time."

"What about Dee?"

"I've got nothing on that one. Nor Jim. Craig . . . the bloody karaoke. And Lisa, she made breakfast if the parties ran on into the morning. Always toast and tea. Fuck."

We're getting somewhere. "What would you say about those who are still alive? And yourself? What methods could they be?"

"Not a clue." He looked up and dropped his hands so they dangled over his knees. "I don't want to think about it all." He bit his bottom lip.

"You should find somewhere else to stay for the time being," she said. "It's your choice, but I'm strongly advising you to do so. Someone is after all of you — you can see that, can't you?"

"I'm going nowhere. I'd like to see someone try to kill me." A boast? Bravado?

Bethany held back a sigh. "It would only be for a few days, until we've caught this person."

He laughed at that. "You're forgetting something. If everyone remaining has to leave, what if it's one of us? Say they stop killing while we're all away, then when we think it's safe to come back, it starts again?"

"The same could be said for if it's someone else," she said. "Say, a neighbour from the other streets."

"Well then, you've proved my point. Why leave? They'll come after us either way."

"Are you sure I can't persuade you?"

"Nope."

They said goodbye and left, Bethany not in any mood to argue with obstinacy and a touch of arrogance. His comment about him liking to see someone kill him . . . He might very well find out what that was like in the near future.

As there was no sight of Presley's car, she let Isabelle know where they were going and then drove them to the pub. Inside, Mike collared the same lady from earlier and ordered them a meal — pie and mash for him, lasagne and chips for her, plus a large coffee each.

Then he asked, "Did Melinda come back in here?"

The barmaid handed over his credit card. "She did. Raging, she was."

"In what way?" Mike ran his finger down his temple.

"Pissed off she's been accused of killing Jim. Is it true he's dead?"

"I'm afraid so," Bethany said. "When did she leave?"

The woman's answer matched the time frame of when Melinda had arrived back in Le Huray. Well, that was one alibi sorted for definite.

They sat to wait for their meals, and Bethany rang Fran. "Anything?"

"We're so swamped with these alibis for those living behind Le Huray that we haven't done much else. Digi did send an email about Amanda's phone and laptop, though. Lots of messages between her and Keith, as you'd expect, but nothing sinister. The calls she made have been verified as innocent."

"Did you get Dee's back yet?"

"They said tomorrow morning."

Bethany told her what had been going on. "Unless those transcripts had anything to do with the methods of death in them, go home. If you're not getting anywhere, it can wait. Get some rest and thank you for your work today."

She ended the call just as their food was brought over. "Can you make up about twenty baguettes to take out?" she asked the server. Okay, probably too many, but she hadn't tallied up how many officers were in Le Huray and in the copse, and to be honest, couldn't be bothered.

"Can do. What fillings?"

"Best just stick with cheese. Thanks."

Tucking into her dinner revived Bethany somewhat. For a short while she was just normal, a woman out with her work colleague. She pushed the day out of her head, and between bites, they talked about life in general, plus Bethany's rotary washing line and whether she'd need concrete to secure the spike that held the pole.

The mundane in life still went on with death all around them.

The coffee helped perk her up some more, and they collected the baguettes between them, paid and walked out.

"I won't be a sec. You may as well wait in the car." Bethany stood at the end of the alley to the copse. She got Penny's attention, and the uniform walked down to meet her. She handed over the right amount of food after Penny told her how many people were in the copse. "Has Jim been collected?" she asked.

"Any time now."

"Okay. See you soon."

"Thanks for the food."

Bethany waved and got back in the car. In Le Huray, Presley had parked on the road adjacent to Dee's. Lisa's was the first port of call so they could talk to him. On her way across, Bethany made a mental note that Melinda's car still sat on her drive, but Sarah's and Bob's wasn't there, the same for Jane's. Relieved those three were away and out of immediate danger — who knew if the killer would work out where they'd gone and follow them there; that might mean putting them all up in hotels instead — Bethany handed the baguettes to a random uniform and asked him to give them out. She togged up along with Mike, signed the log that a uniform she didn't know held out for her, then entered Lisa's and met Isabelle on the landing. Mike went into the bathroom with Presley, the brave bugger.

Presley told them what they already knew — the roundabout time of death.

"I'm done here," he said. "So shall we go over to Craig's?"

Bethany nodded. "I gather Sarah, Bob and Jane have left."

"Yes, I said that was fine," Isabelle said. "Jane's gone to her own home — I guessed Fran and Leona would have her address. Melinda is digging her heels in about staying put."

"So you spoke to her then?"

"I did, and she definitely wants to stay."

"Funny, so does Keith . . ."

Isabelle's eyebrows arched. "It could be the pair of them, you know. It might be one of those sick sex games."

Mike came out of the bathroom. "I watched a documentary about a couple who did that."

"Oh God," Bethany said. "You've set him off now." She laughed.

"No, seriously. This bloke wanted a woman who'd help him kill. He'd planted it in her head over the course of a year or so, and in the end, she agreed to do it. She was infatuated with him. So off they went, on a mad spree."

"Where was this?" Bethany asked.

"America. The thing is, the docu was only on the week before last. They could have got the idea from that if they watched it. Keith's a bit emotionless — a classic sociopath trait. They lack empathy, like he seems to. Their relationships are meaningless, and given what Keith's been up to with other women, that's another tick in a box for him as a narcissist, so it wouldn't bother him to kill them."

"What about her, though? She's bloody awful." Bethany shuddered. "Highly strung, I'd say, not to mention a cow."

"She's just going along for the ride?" Mike shrugged. "Infatuated with him so will do whatever he asks? Myra Hindley and Ian Brady, anyone?"

"With the other neighbours gone, they'll only have each other to kill," Bethany said.

"Bib-bib," Presley said, waiting for them to move then walking between them and going downstairs.

Bethany, Mike, and Isabelle followed, signing out of the scene and into the one at Craig's, all with new booties and gloves on.

"Is that someone with grub?" Isabelle all but pounced on the uniform in Craig's kitchen. "I'll eat that in a mo. Bloody starving. Did you fork out for them?" she asked Bethany.

She nodded. "You can buy the next meal. You got breakfast too, remember."

"Ah, the manky bacon rolls."

"I'll let you go without in future."

"Can you two stop gossiping?" Presley called from beside Craig in the living room.

Suitably chastised and pulling faces at each other, Bethany and Isabelle joined him, as did Mike. Craig's estimated time of death was before Lisa. Presley's prediction was *so* close to the hour they'd spoken to Craig about why he thought Melinda might have chosen him to call about Jim's death.

"We could have literally walked out of here while someone walked in the back," she said.

"Not our fault." Mike gave her a stern look, his usual warning for her not to torment herself with it. "Craig was alive when we left him. He said his back door was locked when we asked about it and advised him to keep safe."

All the same, it didn't make Bethany feel any better. "I want to go over and check on Melinda. Who knows if she's been murdered while we've all been right here in the close. If we get nowhere with her, I'm going home."

"Lucky shit," Isabelle said. "I still have to clear the scenes, get the bodies collected. I won't see my bed this side of midnight."

Bethany refused to feel bad. Their jobs required different things. Isabelle didn't have to gad about questioning people, which was mentally exhausting, although she could pass the scenes on to another of her rank, except she chose to work on and see it through until the end.

"But first, I'm going to eat this magnificent beast." Isabelle stared down at the baguette in her gloved hand, smiling.

Out the front again, Isabelle standing in the street to scoff her head off, Bethany led the way to Melinda's. Mike knocked, and Melinda swung the door open.

"I saw you at Keith's," she spat, as though they'd committed a sin by going there. "Did he tell you why he hasn't answered my messages?"

"Let's go inside, shall we?" Bethany glared at her.

Melinda stepped back and let them in, then closed the door and took them into the kitchen. "Well? Did he?"

"We weren't there to discuss your messages," Bethany said, although she wished she *had* asked him. She'd have got an insight into how he was feeling about her now they'd been caught out in their cheating. If he was ignoring her texts and calls, it sounded like he didn't want anything to do with her.

"So what *did* you want with him then?" Melinda parked a hand on her skinny hip.

None of your sodding business. "We're here to ask you to leave the close for a few days, for obvious reasons."

"No. Not without Keith."

"You'll be the only two left. Easy pickings."

"I don't care."

"So this isn't serious enough for you to find somewhere safe to go for a while?" Bethany asked. "Do you *want* to be killed? Our officers aren't going to be here indefinitely."

Melinda rolled her eyes. "This is boring me. I want you to leave. If I get scared, I'll go to Keith's."

Bethany doubted any amount of persuasion would change the woman's mind, so they left her to it and went to sit in the car.

They talked everything through.

"Rather than go home, we should chat to the Casprey lot again," she said. "I'll collect a couple of uniforms from here."

She got out of the car and organised that, then they were off up the alley beside Keith's. Like before, they split up, and Bethany went straight to David Chesterfield's. He opened the door holding a pen and clipboard in one hand.

"Hello." He smiled.

"Sorry to disturb you again, but there have been some developments in Le Huray, and I wondered if you heard or saw anything, specifically at the homes directly behind you, numbers one to four."

"I would have called if I did," he said, giving her an admonishing look, one he probably bestowed upon his students. "I'm afraid I slept all afternoon. Woke up about ten minutes ago, actually. What's going on?"

He didn't seem off to her at all, so she ignored his query and said, "Thanks for your time." Leaving him open-mouthed and seeming a tad confused, she walked to Elaine Wilson's.

"Oh, has something else happened?" Elaine asked, glancing up and down the street, cheeks paling.

"It has. Did you hear or see anything after I last saw you?"

"I didn't. I stayed indoors, everything locked up. I'm just about to go and stay with my son, like I told you. I couldn't go any earlier because he was at work." She pointed to a suitcase in the hallway.

"A very good move. I'll leave you to it."

Other houses on Bethany's list hadn't seen anything either, so she walked to the one beside David's. No answer. At the one next to that, she rang the bell.

"We were at my mother-in-law's all day," a man said. "We go every Sunday. Want her number so you can check?"

He gave it, and Bethany wrote it down.

"What about that house?" She indicated the one between his and David's.

"Oh, they're on holiday. Yesterday. Caribbean cruise, by all accounts. Three weeks. Lovely, eh?"

She agreed and left him to his evening, meeting up with Mike, who'd got through his residents quickly. Once again, they helped the uniforms on the other side, and with an hour spent talking to everyone, they hadn't got anywhere.

They all trooped through the alley and back into Le Huray.

Glad to be sitting in the car again, Bethany dropped Mike off at his place then went home. She sent Fran an email for tomorrow to ask her to check that man's alibi of being at his mother-in-law's, then had a shower, washing the grime of summer and death off her skin.

Shame she couldn't scrub her mind the same way.

CHAPTER SEVENTEEN

The morning had been a fraught one for David, full of inconvenient hiccups. He'd spilt coffee down his light-blue shirt first thing upon reading an article in *The Shadwell Herald* online. No amount of dabbing at it with a sponge from the staffroom sink had cleaned it. In lesson two, when he'd sat in for Alan, who was running late, a girl had singed her eyebrow with a Bunsen burner flame, and David had just about had a heart attack at the lad who'd slapped her face thinking she was on fire. At lunch, he'd slid on a chewed-up gummy sweet a student had spat out, much to the pleasure of a few kids hanging around at the lockers. All in all, he was pissed off and uptight, especially with what he was doing later after work. It brought on some anxiety, which was alien considering he'd managed to kill the others without getting nervous.

He should have finished them all off yesterday while he was in the right mindset.

With a free period this afternoon where he was supposed to be planning out next week's lessons, he opened his laptop and visited the news site again to see if they'd added anything to it.

LOCAL RESIDENTS MURDERED!
WHO IS INTENT ON OBLITERATING THE QUIET CLOSE?
PETER UXBRIDGE — REGIONAL CRIME

If you thought Shadwell was safe after the spring murders this year, think again. As usual, our trusty source at the police station has informed us of something quite disturbing. Residents of Le Huray Close have been killed one by one in a matter of hours over the raging-hot weekend, all in different ways. Does that mean multiple killers are at large or that one person is incredibly inventive? With heavy police presence at the close after the first murder, it makes us wonder how the killer managed to get to the others. Our source said:

"We have an extremely bold individual on our hands, one who has managed to commit terrible crimes while officers have been in the vicinity. This is not to say our policemen and women haven't been paying attention, but that the culprit is fearless in his or her pursuit and has managed to outwit us."

All residents are friends and have known one another for years. It makes you wonder, doesn't it, whether one of them has a beef with the others, but that's just speculation at this point in time, although it bears a striking resemblance to the Obbington case where several members of a friendship group were eliminated — on our very own doorstep, no less.

Has Shadwell become a place where people feel it's okay to do what they want? Since the Collier case, involving DI Tracy Collier, who, incidentally, scurried miles away to head the Serious Crimes Squad when everything blew up, distancing herself from Shadwell, our beloved place has deteriorated, although word has it that Collier also has a heavy murder workload. Did that case set the precedent? Considering the amount of serial killers we've had in our midst of late, one has to wonder . . .

The Le Huray residents who have had their lives cruelly snatched away include Amanda DeBord, Dee Groocock, Jim Ody, Craig Gillan and Lisa Hicks. I have it on good authority that the manner of deaths are as follows: A slit throat, choking by food, strangulation using rope, suffocation with a microphone, and electrocution via a toaster in the bath. What sort of person thinks of all these things? The remaining homeowners, Keith Trannor, Sarah and Bob Hodgson, Jane Vanes and Melinda Nash, must be worried out of their minds. Wouldn't you be?

What's next? Someone being gassed? Arson? The mind boggles.

We urge you to lock your doors, day and night, and be vigilant.

If anyone has any information regarding this case, please contact us, Chief Kribbs at Shadwell station, or Crimestoppers.

We'll update you with the latest as and when it comes in. Stay tuned!

An extremely bold individual. Although David liked that term, he'd have preferred another word. Yes, he was bold, but he was weary, and enough was enough. The very police he'd killed under the noses of were the ones responsible for allowing those bloody parties to continue. If they'd nipped them in the bud during year one, everyone would still be alive.

His performances being in the news was disturbing. He hadn't thought about this aspect of his actions. It had hit him this morning that what he'd done was newsworthy, of course it was, hence him checking the *Herald*, but to see it down in black and white . . . Discomfiting. He'd seen it as a job to be done to make himself and his Casprey neighbours happy. A service. A kindness. But the article had given him something else to think about. Shadwell would be living in fear. That wasn't his aim.

He should have known he wasn't cut out for the harsher aspects when he hadn't liked seeing his victims after he'd silenced them. What a walking contradiction he was. A therapist's dream. Someone they could analyse. He wasn't a sociopath or a psychopath, just a man driven to the edge by inconsideration, righting the wrongs.

What *did* that make him then? There had to be a label.

He searched for the story in other places, shocked further to find it had hit the *national* news. Oh. This wasn't good. What if journalists turned up at Le Huray? In Casprey? How would he get to the others with more people around to spot him?

Fucking hell. All he wanted was a quiet life.

Alan popped his head around the door, and David jumped. He quickly erased his search history, hand shaking. You never knew who'd nose when you weren't around, did you, poking about in your personal browsing.

"What can I do for you?" David asked.

Alan plonked himself behind one of the student's desks, the chair groaning. "Did you see the news?"

David shook his head. "No . . ." *Liar.*

"You live by Le Huray Close." Alan had dropped him home once when David's car had decided not to start, so he must have remembered from that.

"And?"

"People have been murdered there." Alan slapped the desk to punctuate his statement, eyes widening then narrowing suspiciously.

Has he put two and two together?

"I know." David nodded, sage as you like. "The police called round yesterday. Twice."

Alan's eyebrows danced about. Slithering beasts, they were. "And you didn't tell me because?" He cocked his head.

"Well, it's all a little" — he pinched a word from his earlier thoughts — "discomfiting."

"And the rest! What did the police say?" Alan leant back, settling in for the duration, for fuck's sake, arms folded over his orange Hawaiian shirt that the kids all took the piss out of. Going on holiday, sir? Got one of those flowery necklaces to go with it, sir?

Bloody great, he wants details. "Obviously, they asked if I'd seen or heard anything. I hadn't, so they went on their way."

"What, that's it? But those people were killed *behind your house*, Davey."

He hated being called Davey. It annoyed him something chronic. He had the mad idea to add Alan to his silence list. He'd have a *really* quiet life then, apart from that annoying pair of lads who sat at the back of the class disrupting everyone else. *No. No killing kids*. "Afraid so." He had to get rid of Alan and get him to leave the room. While David had questioned him in the past about how he felt about mass killings, now he'd actually done it, talking about it wasn't high on his list of priorities.

Offing the rest without being caught was.

"Do you believe in anticipating incidents?" Alan tucked his hands behind his head.

"What do you mean?" A worm of nervousness writhed about in David's gut, reminding him of that bloody gummy sweet earlier. That had been a worm, too.

"Like, you know, when you asked my opinion on mass murder that time . . ." Alan sneezed. "Ruddy hay fever. I swear to God it gets worse every year. So yeah, what do you think about what I said?"

"You mean predicting the future?"

"That's it."

"Why would I believe in that?" The only way he'd predicted it was by planning it, not that he was some kind of freaky guru.

"Well, you mentioned it, and now it's happened, albeit not at school." Alan dipped his head in a knowing gesture.

Does he suspect it's me? "Err, I think you're away with the fairies."

"Not really. You wanted to discuss it, and now it's going on in the street near you."

"Hardly the same. We were talking about assault rifles and the like. Besides, I wanted to discuss it because of the *children*." David harrumphed for effect. "I *told* you it was all about what was going on in America. I want our students to be safe, and in order to do that, we set up the chats with the kids we thought were likely to commit such an awful thing *if* they weren't shown they could overcome their hang-ups."

"Fair enough, it's just been bugging me ever since I read that article this morning, that's all."

"What exactly are you saying, Alan? That I talked about it, therefore, I'm responsible for what's occurring in Le Huray?" David laughed. "You always did have a vivid imagination."

"What are you on about?" Alan lowered his hands to his lap and sat forward, banging his knee on one of the desk legs. "Ow!"

"Your alien theory, for example. 'They live among us.' That's what you said."

Alan got all flustered and shot to his feet. "I've got work to do."

"So do I . . ." David raised his eyebrows. "Have fun thinking about meeting an extraterrestrial, mate."

Alan stormed out, red-cheeked.

That'll teach him to fling accusations about.

David chuckled. Some people were just weird.

CHAPTER EIGHTEEN

Monday had dragged so far. The team were no closer to finding who had done this. Dee's devices had been checked by digi, and just like Amanda's, nothing sinister had been picked up. Now they just had to wait for Jim's, Craig's and Lisa's. There had to be something, somewhere, didn't there?

Bethany had retreated to her office after lunch to get on with the paperwork. Strong afternoon sunlight blasting in through the window behind burnt her back, and she got up, going over there intending to lower the blind. She caught sight of Nicola leaving to start her shift on foot, and an attack of the guilts gripped her.

She shouldn't have encouraged them to cover up what Nicola had done.

But if she hadn't, Kribbs could have accused Bethany of not working the scenes properly and insisted Tracy Collier and Damon Hanks from Serious Crimes came to assist.

Bethany had been to his office this morning to update him on what was going on. A bear with a sore head didn't cover it. After she'd told him the details, he'd basically ignored it and launched into a tirade about his wife, who'd left him recently, getting her solicitor onto him about money. She wanted some — a lot, actually — for putting up with his absence over the years while his career had held him in its grip. She'd played the card of being a lonely wife, a widow to the force. For him to know about the balls-up with Nicola . . . No, he was in a bad enough mood as it was.

She convinced herself again that she'd done the right thing.

No more guilt. It was too late to retract it. She'd deal with any fallout later.

Antsy and in need of getting out of the station, she left her office and collared Mike, who'd just signed off on his statements on the case so far.

"Fancy a drive?" she asked.

He looked up and squinted. "Where to?"

"Let's go and see Vicky Trannor again. I realised that while we'd questioned her about Keith, we hadn't asked her what *she'd* been doing over the weekend. We got called away before we could conclude the interview."

"What, you think she's disgruntled with them all because they locked her out of the Le Huray clique after she left Keith?"

"It's not fantastical," she said. "People kill for the slightest of reasons, you know that."

"Fair enough." He shut his computer down and popped his paperwork in a beige file.

"Carry on poking into the deep past of all the residents," she said to Fran and Leona. "You never know, something might pop up. We're off to Vicky Trannor's, then we might swing by Casprey again, just to see if anyone who was out before noticed anything going on. I'm curious as to why none of the others have been bumped off overnight or today." She frowned. "Unless it's Keith and Melinda, and with the others gone, there's no one for them to murder."

"Hmm," Leona said, "but they'd know where Jane lives, wouldn't they? Plus where Sarah and Bob's son is. If they're as matey as they sound, that is."

"Maybe they're only comfortable killing in their own environment," Fran suggested.

"It just seems odd no one else is dead," Bethany said, "if we're going on the assumption one of them has it in for the rest. Whatever, we'll have to keep plodding on until we've exhausted all avenues."

"By the way, I just wrote this on the whiteboard, but the CCTV checks I did yesterday and earlier haven't thrown anything up," Leona said. "No cameras anywhere near Le Huray, just the one outside the row of shops on the other side of the estate, which point at the car park. All vehicles seen entering it have been verified as genuine and just going there to nip into the chemist or Tesco Express. I requested in-store footage from both places, and they were more than happy to provide it. Today I've gone through the lot, and everyone spotted in the car park went into the shops. We can't prove one way or another whether they went home again afterwards or visited Le Huray because of there being no cameras on the estate, so I could have spoken to our killer and not known it."

"Frustrating," Bethany said. "I know I always grumble about it, but it's also frustrating that Uxbridge got hold of the story and has splashed it in the news."

"Um, it's gone national since you last saw it," Fran said.

"Wonderful." Bethany shut her eyes for a moment. "Let's hope they're not all camped out at Le Huray. We'll have a look while we're in the area."

"Melinda Nash has spoken to them." Fran cringed.

"Oh, bloody hell, that's all we need. Get it up on your screen for me, will you?" she asked Mike.

LE HURAY RESIDENT SPEAKS OUT!
PETER UXBRIDGE — REGIONAL CRIME

Melinda Nash, of Le Huray Close, has told us of the terror she experienced finding her boyfriend, Jim Ody, dead in the copse by The Fox and Grapes on the Warburg estate.

"Oh, it was awful," she said. "I went to meet him at the pub where we always have our Sunday dinner, but he'd been and gone. I checked the copse as we walk through there afterwards, every week without fail, and sit on the stones on the grass. He'd been strangled with a rope against a tree."

Asked how the deaths of Jim and those of her friends had affected her, she said, "I'm inconsolable. I can't believe it's happened. We were all so close. You know, best friends. And now half of them are gone, and I've lost the love of my life."

"The love of her life, my arse," Bethany said once she'd finished the article, which was more of Melinda waxing lyrical about how much she loved Jim and that it wouldn't be the same without him and her neighbours. "She jumped into bed with Keith quickly enough."

"I wonder if he's ditched her since we last saw them," Mike said, "which is why she's lapping up the attention Jim's murder brings her."

"Wouldn't surprise me." Bethany shook her head. "She really is gross. She'll be yapping to the nationals next, getting paid for it an' all. Anyway, enough about her. We need to get going."

They left the station, and Bethany drove to Vicky's. Inside, with them all seated around the kitchen table, she got straight to the point.

"I didn't get a chance to ask the rest of my questions yesterday, so we've just nipped back to do so now. It's standard, so don't be alarmed, but what were you doing over the weekend?"

"I was at my mum's with my son, Toby," she said.

Toby was out of earshot in the living room, colouring in. He was the image of Keith and looked to be around four.

Shite. So it isn't her then. "Where does she live?"

"Mablethorpe. Mum has a cottage there. It's handy, because it isn't far away, and Toby likes the beach. The locals hire a community hall every so often, and there's a party, so we went to it and had a lovely time."

Lots of witnesses. "That sounds wonderful. We also didn't touch on how you feel about those in Le Huray basically freezing you out. Why would they do that, do you think?"

"Keith's the one who puts up with them at his place for the parties, so it stands to reason they stuck by his side. It's to their benefit, after all." Vicky rolled her eyes. "While I liked them when I lived there, it was clear that once I'd gone, out of sight, out of mind came into play. I never went back. When Keith has Toby, he has to come and pick him up here. He's due to have him later, actually, and I'll be stressing to him that he mustn't take Toby to his house, for obvious reasons."

"I'm glad you said that, because I was about to suggest the same thing. To be honest, is it ideal for Keith to have him at the moment? If he takes him out, he risks something happening — what if he's being followed? — and if he brings him here, he risks danger coming to your door."

Vicky shuddered. "For all I know, I could be in danger anyway because I lived in Le Huray before."

True. If someone had a problem with everyone who had ever lived there, more bodies might show up in different places.

"Excuse me for just a second." Bethany tapped out a message to Fran to look at past residents and speak to them. She put her phone away and smiled. "Is it possible for you to go back to Mablethorpe for a while? I'm sure if you need us to speak to the school about taking Toby out early before the summer break, they'd be amenable in the circumstances."

Vicky held her fingers to her lips. "Oh. You think . . . Jesus Christ!" She nodded. "I'll pack now. There's no way I'm putting Toby at risk. Will you stay until I've done it?" She stood. "You've scared me now."

"Please be quick. We need to get moving really."

While Vicky dashed out and up the stairs, Bethany read the message she'd just received.

> Fran: DIDN'T YOU SEE IT ON THE WHITEBOARD? EVERYONE WHO LIVES THERE HAS DONE SO SINCE THE HOUSES WERE BUILT. THE ONLY ONES WHO

AREN'T THERE NOW ARE VICKY TRANNOR, HER SON, AND SARAH AND BOB'S SONS.

Bethany: OKAY, THANKS.

She related that nugget to Mike. "So with Vicky going to her mum's," she said quietly, "that lessens fatalities."

She messaged Fran again.

Bethany: CAN YOU RING SARAH AND ASK HER IF IT'S POSSIBLE FOR THEM ALL TO GO TO A HOTEL OR SOMETHING — HER, BOB, HER SONS AND ANY IMMEDIATE FAMILY HER BOYS HAVE — WIVES, GIRLFRIENDS, CHILDREN. THEN GET HOLD OF JANE AND DO THE SAME FOR HER. TELL THEM WE WANT TO KEEP THEM SAFE FOR THE TIME BEING.

She passed that on to Mike. "Then we'll only have Keith and Melinda to worry about, stubborn pair of bastards that they are, although with Melinda talking to the paper, making out she's devastated, maybe she'll reconsider leaving Le Huray now she clearly isn't interested in Keith. I'll let Fran have the pleasure of dealing with her." She sent a third message.

Vicky appeared then, trailing a large, wheeled suitcase behind her. She grabbed a phone charger from a drawer, stuffed it in her handbag, and said, "Right, all ready. Ah, hang on. Just need to lock the back door." She did that, then vanished out into the hallway.

Bethany and Mike followed. Vicky finished off putting trainers on Toby, then slipped on a pair of ballerina flats — her feet were tiny.

"Where are we going, Mummy?" Toby frowned and looked up at his mother.

"Back to Nanny's."

The boy danced about, and Vicky opened the front door. Mike lugged her case to her car, putting it in the boot, and Bethany closed the front door behind them.

"I'm not telling Keith where I am," Vicky said from the driver's seat, leaning over to peer out of the passenger window.

"Probably for the best. Contact the school. Tell them to get hold of me if they have a problem." She handed Vicky a card in case she'd left the last one she'd given her in the house. "What's your mum's address?"

Vicky gave it, and Mike wrote it in his notebook, then she revved the engine and drove away.

"That's them safely dispatched." Extreme relief winged its way through Bethany. The thought of that kiddie being caught up in all this . . . "Now to Casprey. We'll keep it brief and speak to the residents directly in front of Le Huray for now, although they'll most likely be at work."

That proved to be the case, a wasted trip, although Fran messaged back to say all of the Hodgsons were going to stay in the Travelodge, and Jane would be joining them later — she'd had to go to the doctor this morning to get sleeping tablets. She hadn't slept a wink last night mourning her sister. Melinda had also agreed to leave, so that just left Keith, and she didn't bother trying to persuade him again. He'd been adamant he wouldn't leave.

By the time they got back to the station, five o'clock had rolled around. Bethany sent Fran and Leona home, then she added more to the whiteboard regarding their interview with Vicky.

"Want me to sort that rotary line out for you?" Mike asked. "We could nip to Homebase and pick up some quick-drying cement."

"I can do it," she said. "But thanks for the offer."

"Want to be alone, do you?"

"It's not that, just . . . I need to learn to stand on my own two feet."

"That's a shame. I was going to ring for a takeaway delivery while I was at it."

"Well, now you've said that . . . But I still want to sort the line myself."

"Fine by me. I'll sit and watch."

"And no offering suggestions, right?"

They laughed and left the station, arriving at Bethany's ten minutes later.

God, it was good to be home.

CHAPTER NINETEEN

Keith stared out of the window for the umpteenth time. He hadn't gone to work today and was unable to face it because of the recent shit going down. The bodies of his neighbours had been removed, and he'd watched it all unfold, goosebumps springing on his arms and shivers wiggling down his back. How had this happened? What the hell had they all done to whoever had killed them? He imagined them in morgue fridges, friends in death like they'd been while alive. Was he destined to join the post-mortem queue? Was he stupid to have stayed here, the only one left?

After Melinda had spoken to the papers, he'd texted to tell her it was over. He couldn't hack her constant messages and the phone trilling with her calls. She'd continued bugging him afterwards, so in the end, he'd blocked her number. Who wanted a needy female on top of this crap?

It was silent. Eerie. As though the world had ended, or maybe an apocalypse had occurred and he was the only human left. Would Melinda, Bob and Sarah ever come back, or had they decided to stay away for good, the close too tainted by murder for them to want to return?

Christ. I don't know what to do.

Not one for showing his emotions in situations too hard to handle, he was basically alone in this. Well, apart from those coppers, the man and woman. Maybe he ought to ring them and let them know he was fucking off an' all. A hotel. His mum's in Lincoln. Vicky's.

Toby barged into his head, and he remembered he was meant to be having him this evening. Shit! Once again, he'd been a twat, forgetting the one person he should never forget. He'd planned to take him to the pool, had bought Spiderman armbands, too, and intended to teach the lad to swim. Now it was too late, what with it being eight o'clock. Toby was usually in bed by seven.

He was never going to win the Dad of the Year award.

Sighing, he took his phone out and, still standing at the living room window, called Vicky. She'd rip him a new one, that was a given, but maybe she'd understand, seeing as some killer was going round murdering the neighbours.

"Keith, we're not home," she said. "Sorry, I was meant to ring you and let you know. You're not at mine, are you?"

Seemed he'd got away with this one. "I was, but you weren't in." How easy it was to lie to her. "So I came home again. Thanks for the wasted journey."

"Don't start," she snapped. "I've had a bloody bellyful today. I wouldn't have had to leave if you lot hadn't got yourselves into the biggest pile of shite ever. What the hell is going on?"

So she'd heard. And what did she mean? "Leave? What are you guffing on about?"

"I had a visit from the police."

"What did they need to see *you* for?" He scratched his stubbly cheek.

"Considering I was married to you, they had questions."

His stomach flipped. "What, about me?"

"Who else?"

"Do they think *I* did it?"

"Who knows, but I answered them honestly. Then they came back and asked me where *I* was this weekend. Thank

God I was at Mum's, otherwise they'd be suspecting me. I know I can't stand you and Amanda, but I wouldn't kill you."

"You've said you'd kill me often enough."

"Oh, get lost, that's just something you say. I didn't *mean* it. So we had to leave. The police weren't happy about me and Toby staying around because of our connection to Le Huray."

"They don't think *you'll* get killed, do they? And Toby? Fuck. Where are you?" His life was spiralling out of control. Who would want to bump off a little boy?

"I'd rather not say. That way, if that nutter gets hold of you, they can't torture it out of you, can they. Why have you stayed at home? Are you mental or just the usual stubborn? Do you even *want* to live?"

"Of course I bloody do."

"Then get out."

"I've got nowhere to go except Mum's."

"Go there then! Keith, you're one of the biggest dick-heads I know, but risking your life like this is just ridiculous. You have a son who'll miss you. Think about him instead of yourself for once."

Since Keith had shacked up with Amanda, Vicky had taken every opportunity to kick him in the nuts, but she had a point there. Toby didn't deserve the grief he'd go through if Keith was next on the list.

"All right, all right, keep your ruddy hair on." He hated the fact she was right — like she always was. *Bollocks.* "I'll pack in a sec and ring you when I get there."

"Good. Let the police know as well, otherwise they'll be looking for you, thinking you're dead if they come round and you're not in."

Fair point. "Yep, will do." Plus, if they suspected him, this would give him the opportunity to show them he was nothing to do with this. A killer wouldn't tell the coppers where he was going — unless it was to take the limelight off him. He couldn't win no matter which option he took. "Bye for now."

He shoved his mobile away, the damn thing pulling his tracksuit bottom pocket down. Upstairs, he lugged a large sports holdall out of the wardrobe — Vicky had pinched the nice suitcases when she'd stormed out — and opened the flap ready to put some clothes inside. Within five minutes he'd collected a few tops and jeans, underwear and the like, and walked into the en suite. He stuffed a few things in a toiletry bag and threw it on the bed.

A familiar creak sounded downstairs, and he paused to listen. That noise had always got on Vicky's tits, where the panels of flooring beneath the laminate in the living room rubbed together in the summer, the heat expanding them. Funny how it didn't do it in winter when the heating was on.

Had someone stood on the flooring, or was it just the hot evening swelling the boards?

He lifted a pile of T-shirts and placed them in the holdall.

That creak again.

If someone was in the house, they were a bit thick if they trod on the dodgy bit twice after hearing the noise the first time.

A thump.

What the fuck was *that*?

His heart hammering, Keith grabbed his baseball bat beside the bed then crept out of the bedroom and down the stairs. If an intruder thought they could ambush him, they had another think coming.

* * *

David cursed his bum bag clip coming loose. The bag had thudded to the floor, and he just knew it would have made a noise. With the scuba helmet on, he hadn't heard a thing, but Keith might have.

David retreated to the kitchen and stood beside the fridge freezer, out of sight of the living room. Was Keith coming back down? David had been spying through the hedge prior to using the key under the flowerpot, and Keith had gone upstairs after a phone call.

The falling bum bag might have alerted him to David's presence.

He attached it to his waist, carefully, so the damn clip didn't click loudly into place.

This job would be more difficult than the others. Even with a full night of sleep, he'd need all his strength to do what had to be done. He peered around and glanced through into the living room at the black wooden decorative beams on the ceiling. Was the middle one sturdy enough for what he had in mind?

He clenched his fists and waited.

The end of a baseball bat appeared midair, waist height, so he leapt forward and swung to face Keith. A hard whack to Keith's face had the bloke going down, smacking the back of his head on the floor tiles, the bat leaving his now star-shaped hand to clatter on the kitchen floor and then roll to rest against a cabinet. David's breathing sped up, and he raised a foot to stamp his heavy boot on Keith's face. Then again. Again. After ten, Keith was out of it, and David lost no time in carrying in his sturdy, wide-runged stepladder. He'd practised at home, climbing it with a huge sack of spuds on each shoulder, and reckoned he had this down pat.

Going back into the kitchen, he secured a rope around Keith's neck, leaving a good length for tying the other end where he'd planned. He gripped Keith under the armpits and dragged him into the lounge, avoiding looking at his smashed-up face. He took a deep breath, readying himself for the masterpiece of his life. Bending at the knees, he hefted Keith over his shoulder, mindful the long-haired prat might wake up any second. He gripped the sides of the ladder and climbed, slowly, his face sweating, the inside of the helmet hot and humid.

Concentrate!

Three steps up, and he swayed — Keith was heavier than he looked, and a bag of potatoes did not a body make. He drew on all his strength and made it halfway up, exactly where he needed to be. Now for the awkward bit. He let go of the ladder and felt around for the end of the rope, then reached out to tie it to the large ceiling fan where it was screwed into the beam. If it gave way once he let Keith go . . .

Several knots later, David eased Keith off him, allowing him to dangle, turning away so he didn't see what was happening to the man. David climbed down.

Now that's a fan for you, Keith. Better than your bloody neighbours any day.

He switched on the living room and kitchen lights, then walked out with the ladder, locked the back door, and replaced the key beneath the flowerpot, all the while expecting the sound of a crash to permeate the helmet where Keith's weight had tugged the fan from the ceiling. He exited via Keith's gate and walked up the alley to his own, entering his garden where he hid the ladder beside the hedge, then kept to the perimeter near the fence and soldier-crawled up the incline to his house.

With the nights being so light, he had to be careful of being spotted, so while still on the ground, he took off his helmet and then went inside, stashing it away in his wardrobe. He peeked out of the back window at Keith's, the view sublime. Keith hadn't fallen, and any thrashing about he might have done while unconscious or coming round from the shock of the rope pressing against his throat was now over.

Everyone on this side of Le Huray had met their maker.

Melinda, Jane, Sarah, and Bob would have to wait until later.

Darkness was a killer's best friend.

* * *

Eleven o'clock arrived, all black and cloaking, with only the moon and stars to witness David standing in Lisa's back garden once again. Word had spread that the bodies had been removed from the other properties — well, Mrs Omar had proudly announced it this afternoon when David had come home from work.

"Gone, they are," she'd said. "Taken away in unmarked vans. I saw them while I was out walking Puggy. That little sod . . . He shit on the pavement."

"Oh dear." David hadn't wanted to talk about that. "So how do you know the vans had bodies in them?"

"Well now, I went round there, didn't I, on the pretence I was taking the dog to the field. Those journalists were there, and they told me."

"Journalists?"

"They were standing at the entrance to the close. Once the vans and the police left, so did the press. Those poor people. Who would *do* such a thing?"

Me.

David let himself into Lisa's, hoping Jane would be in bed. Things would go smoothly if she was. She needed to be there to fit with the plan. Jane always ditched the parties early, claiming tiredness and that midnight was her cue to leave.

"Like Cinderella," Jim had joked once.

Hmm.

David patted his bum bag to ensure the tiara was still in there. Cinderella had one of those, and it would look nice perched on Jane's head. He'd bought it in Claire's Accessories, the winter of year three, so he'd had his woollen mittens on while handling it. He also had a small, clear plastic shoe, and he intended to shove it where the sun don't shine.

He prowled the house, knowing his way around from the last time he'd been here. Upstairs, he averted his gaze from the bathroom, not wishing to see evidence of what had happened in there and walked to the spare room.

The extension lead was no longer plugged in or snaking out onto the landing. It must have been taken for evidence.

Jane wasn't in the bed.

He glanced at the window and, with the curtains closed, flicked the light on to double-check. Where was she?

He crept around the whole house.

Empty.

Bewilderment surged through him. Downstairs, he stupidly opened the broom cupboard to see if she was hiding, then told himself off for it. It was clear she'd left — there wasn't a dog either. Had her husband come back early because of Lisa, and Jane had gone to her own house? That was the logical explanation, but what was David meant to do now? He had no clue where she lived. The conversations at the parties hadn't revealed that.

He left, locking up and then moving on to Melinda's. She wasn't in either, so he mooched in Sarah and Bob's, confused at their absence. This wasn't supposed to happen. Everyone should be dead tonight, then his neighbours in Casprey would get some sleep come the weekend. Now what? He'd have to do some investigating and find out where they could have gone. No one was getting away from him. If they did, the parties would start up again, and even though they'd be held on the other side of the close now Keith was dead, the Casprey folks would still hear it. And new people would come to live in the dead people's houses. What if they were invited to the shindigs?

This would all have been for nothing.

Angry instead of nonplussed, he made his way home via the main road, keeping to the verge, hidden by the trees. At his place, he unpacked his bum bag, tempted to break the tiara to relieve some of his angst.

No. He wouldn't do it. Jane deserved to wear it, and who knew, if her real-life Prince Charming got in David's way, *he'd* be dispatched, too.

* * *

Vicky Trannor was shitting herself. Keith wasn't answering her calls. Okay, he could be driving to Lincoln, running late, but he always used his hands-free, same as she did. Being in control of a car had never stopped him from talking on the phone. He must have taken longer to pack a bag than she'd thought. The stupid bastard. Look how quickly she'd left once she'd understood the implications and how vital it was to stay safe. Why hadn't Keith done the same? Wasn't Toby important enough to stay alive for?

Next, she dialled his house phone.

Still no answer.

There was only one thing for it. She'd have to ring her ex-mother-in-law. Vicky couldn't stand the woman, but she had to find out what was going on. She took a deep breath and connected the call, bracing herself for a difficult conversation.

"What do *you* want?" came the acerbic voice of Nelly Trannor, spite saturating every syllable.

Vicky was surprised Nelly still had her number in her phone to know it was her. She thought it would have been deleted long ago. "Um, is Keith with you yet?"

"Yet? What do you mean *yet*?"

"He was supposed to be coming to yours because of the murders." Vicky fiddled with her mum's sofa cushion. Nelly always got her all nervy.

"What murders?"

"Haven't you heard?"

Nelly sighed loudly. "Does it sound like I bloody well have, you dopey cow?"

Vicky closed her eyes for a second and swallowed, then went on to explain what had happened in Le Huray. "So he was coming to yours, to keep safe."

"Well, he didn't ring to say so, and you know how much I hate it when people just turn up on my doorstep without asking first."

"But he's your son."

"Doesn't bleedin' matter. If I don't want company, I don't want company. He's probably fallen asleep, the lazy git. Anyway, the spare bed isn't made up, so when he gets here, he'll have to do it himself. That's a pest, that is, him doing this. I've got friends coming round tomorrow for a bit of red velvet cake and a natter. The last thing I need is him scoffing it and dropping crumbs on my nice new cream carpet."

How the hell could Nelly not care that her son might be next? What was *wrong* with the woman? "Okay, I'll ring the police instead."

"You dramatic mare. Always been the same, you have. Look at how you ran off when he started seeing that Amanda. Necessary? Couldn't you have stayed around because of Toby? Patched things up?"

"No. Goodbye." She jabbed at her screen to end the conversation. Nelly always had been a strange breed, and Vicky was fucked if she'd carry on chatting with her only to be put down.

She fished out the card Bethany Smith had given her and plugged in the mobile number.

"Hello?" Bethany asked, sounding groggy.

"Sorry to bother you so late, but it's Vicky."

"Vicky Trannor?"

"Yes. I'm worried. Keith agreed to stay away from his place tonight, only he hasn't turned up at his mum's. I rang her, and she had no idea he was coming."

Did Bethany just say 'shit'?

"What time did you speak to him?" Bethany asked.

"Earlier this evening."

"Okay, leave it with me. I'll go round there."

"Didn't he phone you then?" Vicky asked. "I told him to."

"No. Are you safe in Mablethorpe?"

"Yes."

"Good, stay there until you're told otherwise. Bye for now."

With her heart seemingly in her throat, Vicky went upstairs and sat on the bed. Toby was asleep on a blow-up on the floor, his mouth parted, soft breaths seeping out. God, how would she tell him if something happened to his daddy?

She let the tears fall.

CHAPTER TWENTY

Bethany had called Ursula on the front desk to organise a couple of uniforms to meet her and Mike at Keith's. Now, she waited outside Mike's — he hadn't stayed over after they'd had the takeaway, and she'd successfully cemented in her washing line with no help from him. She was proud of herself but at the same time sad. That was a job Vinny would have done had he still been alive. She'd have sat at the patio table and chatted to him about her day while he worked. Mike had been a poor substitute, much as she loved him.

God, she missed her husband.

Swiping at a tear — damn that grief for sneaking up on her — she smiled through the driver's-side window at Mike coming down his path. Her best buddy looked tired.

He got in and pulled his seat belt into place. "Shame you had to come here again tonight. You only dropped me off an hour ago."

She pulled away from the kerb and drove off. "Yep, and being called out the wrong side of midnight pisses me off. I'd just fallen asleep after my mind finally stopped wittering on about the case. Still, we can't not go, not with what's happened so far. Okay, Keith could have gone somewhere other than his mother's, but Vicky said he was going to ring me — I presume to tell me where he'd be. He didn't."

"Shit."

"That's what I said when she spoke to me." She rounded a corner and headed for Le Huray. "Uniforms are on the way. I left Isabelle. No need to ring her if this is a false alarm."

"Makes sense. Thank fuck the other neighbours left the close." Mike ran a hand down his face. "Blimey, I shouldn't have had that beer. My head's groggy."

"It was only one."

"Hmm."

"Unless you chugged more at your place."

"Nope."

She approached Le Huray. A patrol car had parked across the entrance, and a small van was on the road close to Dee's with no markings on the back to show whether it was a business vehicle. Under a streetlamp, Glen and Tammy appeared in a deep, heated conversation with a dark-haired man who held himself far too upright, giving the impression he was being confrontational. That or he had a rod stuck up his arse.

"That's all we fucking need," she muttered, stopping and then flying out onto the pavement.

The man's voice rose. ". . . and it isn't like I'm doing any harm being here, is it? You're all the same, you coppers, trying to stop a man earning a living. I'm just here to make a few quid, know what I mean? What's the problem with me staying here out of the way?"

"What's going on?" She strutted over to them, brandishing her ID at the bloke, putting it close to his face. "DI Bethany Smith. Problem?"

"The gentleman won't leave," Glen said. "I've asked three times."

"I think you'll find he will." Bethany smiled at the man — barely. "Now, I don't enjoy being out at this time of night dealing with stubborn people, so unless you want me going off on one, piss off before you get arrested."

She walked away, angry, striding to Keith's.

Tammy caught up with her. "I didn't want to say so in front of the reporter, but Keith's dead."

Bethany halted and stared at her. "Reporter? Bloody hell! Did you go inside the house?"

"We didn't need to. Glen stayed with that bloke there, just so he didn't see anything, and I went to Keith's because we really needed to see if he was all right, not argue with a stranger. The lights are on inside. Um, see for yourself . . ."

Bethany took a deep breath and made her way to Keith's. The light was indeed on, and she stepped onto his small patch of grass and looked inside. "Ah, *fuck it*." Frustration bubbled up inside her, and she wanted to scream.

"No stool, no chair knocked over," Tammy said.

"I wouldn't have thought this would be a suicide anyway, what with everything else that's been going on. When his ex-wife rang, I knew what we'd be dealing with, just didn't want to believe it. He was going to stay at his mother's. Clearly, he didn't make it out of the sodding house. No point in us rushing inside. It's clear he's a goner." She shook the image of Keith's bloodied and blue-around-the-lips face from her mind and marched back to the close entrance.

"Still here, are you?" she said to the reporter. "You've well overstayed your welcome."

"I can stand here if I want." He stared at her, the light from the streetlamp giving the impression he'd been a bit liberal with the fake tan.

"Not when this is a crime scene, you can't," she said. "Now knob off." She turned to Mike, not caring that she'd been rude to the journalist twice. "Ring Isabelle, please."

He walked away, phone to his ear.

"Now, I suggest you leave, or my colleague here will take you in. Refusing to comply after being asked nicely results in arrest." She stared at the man. "Am I being clear enough, or do you want a demo?"

"I'm going." He held his hands up and backed away.

"I'll stay here until you've driven off," she said. "And if I catch you back here again, you'll see the inside of a holding cell."

He dumped himself in his van, gave her the middle finger, and reversed, tyres screeching.

"What a total gimp," she said. "Now, Glen, your choice. You stay here and Tammy handles the log at Keith's, or you do it the other way round, makes no odds to me."

"I'll stay here and put some tape up." He smiled.

"Cheers." She returned to Tammy. "Okay, you're on the front door log when everyone else arrives."

Tammy nodded.

"However, I'm going inside with Mike, through the back. I'll just get togged up." Bethany legged it to the car and got clothing out of the boot. She'd need to replenish that next time they were at the station.

Mike joined her in getting dressed. "I've phoned Ursula to find out where Keith's mother lives. Lincoln, so that saves us from having to break the news. Isabelle's on the way here. Said she's looking forward to waking Presley up with a phone call."

"She's such a bugger." Bethany zipped the suit up and then slid on booties. "He must be way behind on PMs, the poor love. Too many bodies." Gloves snapped on, she led the way along the close.

They signed in with Tammy, then walked down the side so they could enter the garden via the gate. Using his torch in the alley, Mike flashed it around, but nothing stood out as off. Bethany went into the garden, and once again, Mike did a quick scope of the area, the beam picking up slices of greenery, the patio table and chairs, and the patio itself. She took the key from under the pot and opened the back door. After a check of the house and finding no one but Keith, they stood on either side of his dangling body.

"So, another rope," she said. "Wonder what the significance of that is for Keith and Jim?"

Mike shrugged. "No idea. Probably something only the killer knows."

"We'll ask the fucker when we get hold of them."

"You said 'them' . . . This has got to be a man. No disrespect, but for a woman to hoist him up like this?" He gestured at Keith. "She'd have to be pretty strong."

Bethany stared at him. "Some women are, you know."

"I realise that, but . . ."

"I understand what you're saying. So how did they get him up there?"

"Your guess is as good as mine."

Someone knocked on the front door.

Bethany went to answer it, smiling as Isabelle and her team breezed past.

"Bit of a bummer my lot have already been through this house and will have to do it all over again," Isabelle said. "But the bonus is, Presley is grumpy as fuck, so expect fireworks in a bit." She rubbed her hands, full of glee.

A photographer snapped images of Keith.

Bethany chuckled. "He didn't let you bother him when he was called out for Amanda, so I bet he does the same thing now."

Isabelle pursed her lips. "I'd forgotten about that. But two nights on the trot might make for an interesting conversation, and like I said, he's already grouchy. Near enough bit my head off when I rang him, so I'd say he's not about to keep up the charade of acting like he's not bothered." She stood in front of Keith, raising her mouth mask. "Whoa, he's not a pretty sight. Beaten up before he was hung, I reckon." She cocked her head. "Hang on — ooh, pardon the pun. That's boot sole imprints on his cheek. You see that?"

Bethany moved closer. "Christ." What appeared to be a patterned toe arc had come up as a bruise on his cheek near his temple where there wasn't much blood or broken skin. To the photographer, she said, "Get a close-up of that, will you? Ta."

"So the killer is getting angry?" Mike mused.

"Maybe, or he had to subdue Keith somehow." Bethany nosed about for anything out of place.

"Ah," Mike said, "so you're admitting you think it's a bloke."

"Oh, shh, you." She grinned. "Looks like his nose is broken even more than when Jim walloped him." She eyed his smashed lips. "That had to have hurt."

"With a bit of luck, he was out of it by the time he was hung," Isabelle said. "Elvis will enlighten us."

"What have I told you about calling me that?" Presley said, coming in and glaring at her over the top of his face mask, his ginger eyebrows forming a V.

"You said not to, but I can't help myself." Isabelle's eyes crinkled.

"I can see you're laughing under that mask," he said. "Stop it." He gazed up at Keith. "Nasty. I'm surprised the weight of him didn't pull the fan down."

A whining creak, a crack, and then Keith dropped. Everyone jumped away as he hit the floor. Bethany's heart pounded, and she cursed their luck. A body left in situ told important tales, and now, with him flat on his back, the fan sitting on his chest, the damn scene was ruined.

"Fucking hell," Isabelle griped. "That answers your question, though, Pres. The weight of him *did* pull it down."

"I can see that, thank you." He looked at his protective suit, then at all of them one by one. "I suggest we get changed into new gear in case we have debris particles on us. I'll go and get some."

He trooped out, and Isabelle laughed.

"God, he's so easy to piss off." She stared at the body. "But this has royally screwed things up. Him falling will have displaced minute evidence."

"If there even is any," Bethany said. "Nothing was found in the other houses, unless there's a report I haven't seen. And that wasn't a dig at you."

"Didn't think it was," Isabelle said. "He's still limp." She nodded at Keith. "No sign of rigor yet. Did Vicky say what time she spoke to him last?"

"In the evening."

"So they were here very recently. We're dealing with a clever bugger." Mike put his mask in place. "Maybe someone who watches a lot of CSI stuff on the telly to not leave evidence."

"Or they just got lucky." Bethany sighed. "So can we see Bob doing this? He's the only man left."

Mike shook his head. "He was in a right state after finding Lisa. Seemed too genuine for it to be an act."

"These sorts of people are good, though," Bethany reminded him. "They know how to behave in certain situations. He could have nipped out the back way and gone into Lisa's through her garden."

"But Sarah was around," Isabelle said.

"Maybe she's in on it." Bethany moved to the window and stared across the road at the Hodgson's. "She might secretly hate all their neighbours, and he's the one doing the dirty work."

"Can't see it myself," Mike said. "Sorry."

"Then who?" Bethany propped her hands on her hips.

Presley came back, remaining on the front path. "Here you go."

The three of them went outside with him and changed, then entered again. While the SOCO photographed the body in its new position, Isabelle took Bethany and Mike on a walkaround. In the main bedroom, a partly packed holdall sat on the bed.

"So he intended on leaving, like Vicky said." Bethany used her wrist to scratch her head. The protective cap had her scalp itching.

"So he was disturbed in the middle of the job?" Isabelle walked over to the en suite doorway. "No toothbrush or paste on the sink."

"There's an open toiletry bag by the holdall," Bethany said. "Some deodorant and whatnot in it. He was so close to getting out of here. And there was me thinking it was him doing this. Unless it was and he *did* kill himself somehow."

"Unlikely." Isabelle came to stand beside Bethany.

"And he couldn't have stamped on his own face," Mike said.

Isabelle *hmmed*. "And if he stood on the sofa to tie the rope, that's a bit of a precarious stretch to lean over that far. It isn't close enough to the ceiling fan."

Bethany agreed. "So we'll need to visit Jane, Melinda, Bob, and Sarah to see where they were when Keith was offed. We'll get a time of death estimate first." She went over to the window and peered out. The house directly behind had ground-floor lights on. "Who lives there again?" She pointed.

Mike stood next to her. "Um . . . David Chesterfield. If he's up, he might have seen or heard something."

"Let's check in with Presley so we have a time frame, then go round there."

Downstairs, with the go-ahead from Isabelle, Presley did the temp. "Before eleven p.m., but I'm not prepared to give an exact time at the moment."

"It would be after he spoke to Vicky, obviously." Bethany felt sick. "It's looking like he phoned her, went up to pack, came down here, and someone did the business. Right, let's go to Chesterfield's."

She left via the front, Mike with her, signing out of the scene. They strode up the alley and into Casprey. At David's door, she knocked, hoping to God he'd seen something or a person hanging around so they had a vague description to go on — build, height, that sort of thing.

With no answer, she peeked through the living room window, the room lit by a silver standard lamp with a paper ball shade. A cream sofa, flat-screen TV on a white cabinet. A blue leather chair with studded buttons was farther down, perched at an angle, the front facing the rear garden, as though he sat there and watched the world go by. Other than that, the room was pretty sparse for such a big one that went the depth of the house.

Something caught her eye through the patio doors at the back. Could be SOCO in Keith's garden, but she didn't think so because they were in white. This movement was darker, a black shape blocking out the view through the gaps in foliage in the hedge. Most of that hedge was speckled with light coming from Keith's, but a section wasn't.

"Mike, come here," she whispered.

He moved to stand beside her. "What am I looking at?"

"The hedge at the bottom of the garden. See what I see?"

"Nope."

"Why isn't there light coming through the leaves in the middle section?"

He squinted. "Ah."

"You reckon he's out there nosing?"

"Probably."

"Why not do it from indoors?"

"Let's go and ask him."

They crept down the alley and stopped beside his gate. Mike turned the handle, and Bethany held her breath in case it made a noise.

She leant forward, close to Mike's ear, and said under her breath, "Get your torch ready. I want to see his face when you switch it on."

Then they stepped inside.

CHAPTER TWENTY-ONE

David was entranced by what was going on at Keith's. He'd put the scuba helmet on so he'd be all but invisible to any Casprey neighbours looking out. Watching from indoors just wasn't the same, and besides, he'd stood here like this over the years keeping an eye on the parties, so why not now during the aftermath?

He'd jumped a bloody mile when Keith had dropped from the ceiling and almost spat the oxygen tube out it had surprised him that much. It had taken a fair while for him to calm down from that, and now his breathing was much steadier, creating a soothing sound, a rasping saw that flattened his bristled nerves.

Two people stood beside the body, staring down at it, their clothing marking them out as Scene of Crime Officers. He wondered what they were saying, and whether they were trying to work out how Keith had got himself up so high without a chair, but they'd be pretty dim if they didn't realise it wasn't suicide. So what then? Were they admiring David's achievement? The results of his stamping on Keith's face? He made out a hank of the twat's long hair, splayed out on the floor. If he'd thought it would hold and not rip out of his head, he'd have tied the bastard to the fan with it.

He turned to check the Casprey houses again. A light snapped on right in front of him, blinding him, and he lifted his hand automatically to shield his eyes, his palm slapping onto the Perspex shield. Heart thrumming, he searched his mind for a good enough excuse to be outside in a scuba helmet but came up empty. Shit. Who held the light? He couldn't see beyond the beam, and a white blob danced every time he blinked. Had one of his neighbours spotted him after all?

Then it sank in. Those two coppers had walked out of Keith's living room not long ago, but David had assumed they'd gone upstairs again.

Bollocks. What was he supposed to do now?

CHAPTER TWENTY-TWO

"Take the helmet off," Bethany said.

Chesterfield didn't do it, and she belatedly realised he probably couldn't hear her. What the bloody hell was he doing wearing it anyway? Did he have some kind of fetish or what?

She reached out her gloved hands, clasped it either side and tugged upwards a bit to give him a clue as to what she wanted. He removed the headgear and stood there staring into the torchlight, blinking, his hair messed up, his cheeks bright red.

"Why are you standing in your garden with that on?" she asked.

"Ah, hello. I wear it periodically to get used to it. I'm going diving in the Bahamas during the summer break."

"So you opted to jam it on your head while watching a *crime scene*?" Was this bloke serious? "Who *does* that?"

"Well, me." Blink. Blink. "Can you stop shining that in my face, please?"

Mike lowered the torch so the beam was concentrated on David's black, long-sleeved T-shirt. "We need to speak to you. Probably best we go inside."

"Fine, fine — *if* I can see where I'm going. I've got spots of light in front of me at the moment." David rubbed his eyes. "What on earth's going on in there anyway?"

"I'd have thought that was obvious," Bethany said, "seeing as you've been gawping. Come on."

She waited for him to lead the way up his sloping garden. He entered via a side door, and they stepped into a kitchen that had one spotlight on beneath a wall cabinet. It gave everything a cosy yellow glow. She closed the door behind them.

"Oh, you have *those* clothes on. The white ones." David put his helmet on the worktop and then proceeded to reach over his shoulder to tug a slimline oxygen tank out of a strappy contraption.

What the fuck?

"Have you been in all evening?" she asked him.

"Yes . . . Marking to do again. Busy day at school." He placed the tank beside the helmet.

It reminded her of a Soda Stream gas canister, only bigger.

"How long were you marking?"

"I finished about eleven and settled down to read for a while. Then I noticed movement in the house at the bottom. Saw people dressed like you and gathered what had happened. Thought I'd go outside and have a look."

"At the same time as practising your breathing with the helmet on." *Sorry, too far-fetched for me.* "I don't buy that."

"I don't care what you buy," he said. "It's the truth. What better way to control your breathing while watching something as scary as that? It prepared me for the fear of encountering a shark."

Granted, he had a point, but *really*? "Did you see anything out of the ordinary before the police arrived?"

He shook his head. "Like I said, marking. I'll show you where I sit, if you like. You'll get a better idea of what I can and can't see from my chair." He walked out, crooking a finger over his shoulder.

They followed to find him sitting in the blue leather chair.

"See this?" He drew out a folding table and set it up. Mimed marking books with his head bent. "I get engrossed and sit like this the whole time. It wasn't until I'd finished, popped the table down beside my chair, and looked up that I saw something was going on. Keith is dead."

"Yes, as you've undoubtedly seen." She walked to stand next to him and then squatted to his level, checking what she could observe. The top half of Keith's kitchen and living room were visible, and if David had glanced up earlier, he'd have seen Keith hanging. *Seen the head of the person stringing him up.* "Did you hear anything?"

"No." He dug down the side of the chair between the arm and his leg and brought out a pair of lime-green foam earplugs. "I use these."

Great.

She peered down to David's front window, estimating whether anyone walking by outside could have also seen into Keith's house. She reckoned the distance was too great for anything of significance to be spotted, maybe the vague impression of people, and Keith dangling from the fan could have presented as a shadow, a trick of the light. She walked there and turned to face the back. Here, she made out Isabelle and Presley, but add another few metres on to account for the front garden, and she doubted anyone would be able to fully observe someone murdering Keith.

She sat on the deep windowsill and stared at the floor in thought. Something had been placed beneath the sofa, and the end of it stuck out. A spread of hair? Blonde. Coarse.

Good grief . . .

"Um, what's that?" She stared at Mike to convey to him that he should stay there with Chesterfield. She had an uneasy feeling. The hair was the same colour as Lisa's.

"What's what?" David rose and made to step towards her.

"Stay there, please." She held up one hand, palm facing him, and pointed to the sofa with the other. "Underneath. What is it?"

He stood still, frowning. "I have no idea. I can't see from here."

Again she spoke to Mike with her eyes, then got down on her hands and knees.

Rope. A fucking great coil of it.

She stood, adrenaline prancing through her with heavy feet. "Why do you have rope?"

"I go climbing." David smiled, puffing his chest out as if proud of that fact.

What is he, a sports fanatic?

He cocked his head. "It's not a crime to own rope, is it?"

"Climbing. Where?" She exhaled slowly through her nose in an attempt to calm her raging nerves.

"Urr, Shadwell Hill," he said.

"With *rope*?" She held back a smile. "You need that to climb the hill, do you?" Did she sound as incredulous as she felt? He was having a bloody laugh if he thought she'd fall for that. You could walk up the hill with no help whatsoever. It was steep but not ridiculously so, for Pete's sake.

"I'm practising for when I tackle the bigger ones." He smiled once more.

Was he just weird or spinning her a yarn? She couldn't make him out. "Right, I'm interested to know how you use the rope when you climb that hill."

"Well, I jog to the top and attach it to an iron spike, then run back down and climb it by pulling myself up the rope."

Definitely weird. "Right . . . Would you mind me cutting off a section and taking it with me?"

"Why would you want to do that?" he asked, cheeks going pale.

"Are you denying my request?"

"Of course not, I'm just asking why you need it."

She stood. Stared at him. "To see if it's the same rope used on Jim Ody and Keith Trannor."

He laughed then, if a tad unsteadily, and clutched his stomach.

Then darted towards her at speed, snarling.

She dodged to the right, and Mike leapt at him, barging into his flank and sending him flying towards the sofa. David crashed into the side of it, the momentum shifting the furniture away from the wall. Mike grabbed David's wrists and yanked his arms back, holding them tight at his lower back. Bethany moved to stand behind him and helped Mike haul him upright.

Something glittered beneath the light of the standard lamp. Something metal. Slim. Long.

A fucking blade.

She glanced at Mike, then to the space behind the sofa. He peered around David, eyes widening.

"Why do you have a sword hidden behind your sofa?" she asked, stepping round to stand in front of David.

"To practise with. I'm learning how to fence. And it's a sabre."

"Oh, fuck right off." She glared at him. "You're going scuba diving, climbing, and now fencing. Do you think I'm stupid?"

"I assure you, that's not the case," David blustered.

"Why did you choose a *sabre* and not an épée?"

David shrugged. "I like it."

"Would you mind if we took the sabre and had a good look at it?"

"Why?"

"Answer my question, please."

"Yes, I would mind. It's mine."

"Why did you race towards me just then?"

"I don't know."

"Have you got something to hide?"

"No, I bloody haven't!"

Her phone rang. *Just what I need.*

She unzipped her suit, pulled her mobile out, and swiped to answer.

Ursula.

"Yep."

"Just had a call. Some bloke called Alan Hughes. He's had a funny feeling about his colleague for a while and couldn't keep it to himself any longer."

"Regarding my case?" She held her breath.

"Yes. Someone he works with asked questions about mass killings a few years ago. Wanted to know what Alan thought about them. Alan said it unsettled him, but his colleague gave the excuse he was worried about the kids, hence bringing up the discussion."

"Elaborate."

"School kids who turn to mass kills because of their upbringing."

School kids . . . "Go on."

"Then the Le Huray killings started, and Alan got a bit worried because his colleague lives in Casprey Lane."

"Right . . . Name?"

"A David Chesterfield."

Christ . . . Her body went weak. "Anything else?"

"Mr Chesterfield was acting oddly today."

"In what way?"

"Jumpy. Defensive."

"Thanks. I'll deal with it." She cut the call and pocketed her phone. "Okay, David, Mike is going to keep hold of you for the moment, so you don't take it upon yourself to make any sudden moves again. I have a few questions. Please remain calm."

"What questions?"

"If you keep quiet for long enough, I'll ask them." She took a deep breath. "Why would you discuss mass killings with a colleague?"

He rolled his eyes. "With Alan? Yes, I did that, and like I told him, I was concerned for the children and the UK turning into America where kids open fire on their classmates. We set up a chat service where troubled kids — those who have terrible home lives — can come to talk out their issues rather than bottling it up inside, which could lead to them expressing their anger and desperation in an altogether different, fatal way."

Plausible. "How do you feel about mass murder, David?"

"It's deplorable, obviously."

"What about if, say, one of the kids at school did it — one with an unstable upbringing. Do you feel, if they've been pushed to the edge, that they're justified in what they do?"

"It's not an excuse, but it's certainly understandable. Those forced to the edge do things they wouldn't ordinarily do."

"So you condone it — under the right circumstances."

He clamped his lips shut.

"I'm going to put in for a warrant to search your premises," she said. "Just to rule you out, you understand."

"I don't want you to." He struggled against Mike's hold.

"I don't care what you want." Bethany rang Glen and told him where they were. "Come in via the side gate. The door is unlocked. Ring for a wagon on the way here, please." She swiped her screen. Then to David, "I think we should have a chat down at the station."

"What about?"

"About the current murders."

"What have they got to do with me?"

"Maybe nothing, but we'd like to talk to you just the same. You have rope and a sabre. We have to cover all bases, and in light of you discussing mass kills with a colleague and lurching towards me the way you did — in anger, I might add — I'd rather we interview you in a controlled environment. I'll get you some nice transport, save you using your own petrol."

"This is ridiculous!"

"Perhaps, but I have a job to do, and something isn't right about you, David."

Glen walked in and looked at Bethany. She nodded, and he strode over and cuffed David, then took one arm while Mike held the other.

"Cuffed! What do you need those for?" David peered over his shoulder. "That's a bit over the top, isn't it?"

"You tell me," Bethany said. "I might well fear for our safety. Cuffs prevent you from doing anything silly. Let's go for a little walk."

They left the house. Mike and Glen escorted David into Le Huray, and along the way, Bethany called in for a warrant, not expecting to get it any time soon, but the quicker she asked for it, the quicker they'd be able to sweep his home.

She headed into Keith's after squiggling in the log. Presley shone a light in Keith's eyes while Isabelle looked on. A SOCO placed an evidence marker down by the sofa arm.

"Ah," she said to Isabelle. "We're taking David Chesterfield in for questioning. Waiting on a warrant for his home, so with any luck, you lot can go in there and have a good root around soon. I've stressed the importance of getting into the house as soon as possible, so you never know, it might get fast-tracked. There's rope under the sofa that looks the same as what was used in the murders, and a sabre behind it." She explained how she'd come to find the items. "Plus, he was standing at the bottom of his garden wearing a *scuba* helmet when we walked in there."

Isabelle blinked and lowered her face mask. "Pardon me?"

"You heard me. Says he was getting into practise before he goes on holiday. Swimming with the sharks, would you believe."

"And we're meant to think that's normal behaviour, are we? On your bloody bike."

Bethany told her about Alan Hughes. "So I'm going to speak to him before I interview David. Ursula gave me the bare bones. I'd rather have the flesh and skin to go with it."

"Nice turn of phrase." Isabelle pulled a face. "Has David given you any reason to think it's him?"

"Apart from the rope and sabre, nope, although, like I said, he did dart towards me at one point. Why do that if you've got nothing to hide?"

"True. It's worth a shot. We have nothing else, so you might as well see what you can get out of him."

"That's what I thought. Sorry, but the rope and a sabre . . . too much for me to ignore. It could be innocent, but I'm not prepared to take the risk."

"Why do you think he did it — if it's him?"

"Hopefully he'll slip up, say something that puts him right in the shit, and I'll find out."

She said goodbye and met Mike at the wagon, which had parked up level with Glen's patrol car. David was already inside, and Mike closed the rear door before slapping it to let the driver know he could be on his way.

"He wasn't happy at being put in there," Mike said.

"I don't suppose he was, but better here than in his own street. If he hasn't done anything wrong, him leaving from Le Huray will stop tongues wagging."

"Do you think he's on the level?"

"Do you?"

"I don't know. It's iffy, but he seems so normal, apart from his imagination. That climbing up Shadwell Hill lark almost had me laughing. It's bullshit."

"If it isn't, we'll have egg on our faces — or I will anyway — but I'm not willing to take the chance of leaving him be." She told him about Alan Hughes.

"Bloody hell . . ."

"Exactly. So let's drop in on him, shall we? Then we'll tackle Chesterfield."

CHAPTER TWENTY-THREE

David sat in a holding cell, wondering how the hell it had come to this. He'd been so careful, so bloody clever up until he'd had the crazy urge to stand by the hedge and peer into Keith's. If he hadn't been doing that, he wouldn't have been caught with the helmet on, and if he hadn't been caught in it, he wouldn't have had to come up with that stupid story about practising his breathing. Then the rope tale. Then the fencing.

What the fuck had he been thinking?

You weren't thinking.

He hadn't factored in getting caught. Hadn't allowed himself to entertain the idea. But he could still get out of this. So what if the rope was the same type? Lots of people in Shadwell could own it. And he'd bleached the sabre, so they wouldn't find anything on it. Good luck to them. They'd come up empty and have to let him go.

He thought about Alan. David had gone too far when he'd discussed killings with him, but he'd saved the day by suggesting the chat sessions. Or at least he'd thought he had. Seemed it had been playing on Alan's mind all along, and the stupid bastard had taken it upon himself to call the police.

So much for colleague solidarity.

CHAPTER TWENTY-FOUR

Alan shoved a hand through his hair, nervous that the police were actually here. It had been bad enough ringing them — he'd all but crapped his pants — but now, with a man and woman staring at him across his dining table, he was having second thoughts. What if he'd read it all wrong? What if David hadn't done anything? Facing him at work tomorrow was going to be tough. What the hell would he say to him if the police let him know what he'd said?

"Firstly, thank you for calling us," DI Smith said. "Can you go through it from the beginning, please?"

Alan swallowed. He felt awful but couldn't retract what he'd said, so he may as well plough on. "A few years ago, David expressed his interest in mass killings." He coughed. "Um, he asked me how I felt about it, whether I thought the people who did that kind of thing had just 'had enough'."

"How did you react to that?"

"Well, I was horrified, to be honest. Who wouldn't be, unless you're not right in the head? I tried to brush it off, but he kept on, saying we'd be like America soon and we ought to do what we could for the kids before it got to that stage in our school."

"Do you believe it would?"

"Of course not. We have good kids, for the most part. One or two bad apples, but they're struggling at home, and they come to our chat group. There's been a marked improvement in their behaviour because of it, so David was right to suggest it."

"What changed? What made you phone us? It's after midnight. It kept you awake, I take it."

Alan nodded. "It did. I had a recent conversation with David. About the murders. When I heard it on the news, my mind immediately went to him, and that can't be good, can it. I mean, you don't think of a colleague as soon as you find out about a serial killer. He doesn't even look like one."

"Most of them don't. Go on."

"So I asked him if he'd seen the news. He said no, then went on about the police coming to speak to him. I mentioned the murders being in Le Huray and that the close was behind his house — it struck me as too coincidental." He shrugged. "I don't know, maybe I'm looking into it more than I should."

"No, you did the right thing in contacting us. Do you know David well?"

"So-so. We chat on breaks, nothing major. We don't share secrets or anything like that."

"Do you know if he's going on holiday this summer?"

Why did they want to know? "He said the Bahamas. Something about scuba diving with sharks."

Smith looked crestfallen at that. Why? What was going on?

"I see. What about climbing? Does he do a lot of that?"

Alan laughed. The idea of David climbing anywhere but into his car or up the stairs was hilarious. "Err, no. He's not sporty at all. Unless he's recently taken it up, I can't see him doing that, sorry."

"And fencing?"

Alan forced a smile away. "As in, DIY? He mentioned having someone in to replace the fence between his and his neighbour's garden. Did he end up doing it himself then?"

"Not that kind of fencing."

Nonplussed, Alan took a moment to get what she meant. "Oh. With a sword? *That* sort of fencing?"

She nodded. "He owns a sabre. Said he liked practising with it."

Alan's blood ran cold. The papers had said that the first woman had been murdered with a blade. Well, a slit throat implied that. Another had been choked, one strangled with rope, and there'd been an electrocution. Could David be capable of that? They said you didn't really know people until you lived with them, but . . .

"I don't think he's the type to do fencing." The thought of David in one of those white outfits, and that mesh head-gear almost had him chuckling, but this wasn't a laughing matter, and he ought to keep himself in check. They might not take him seriously if they thought he found it funny. Nerves played a part in his reactions. It wasn't every day you wondered if your workmate had murdered his neighbours. "He's never mentioned it at any rate."

"Is there anything about him that makes you uneasy?"

"Now you mention it, yes. I've always felt wary around him. Oh, he's a nice enough bloke, don't get me wrong, pleasant and whatever, but there's an edge to him."

"What do you mean by that?"

Alan cast his mind back a good few years. "Take the parties, for instance. Never seen a man get so irate about people having a good time. All right, they're a bit noisy, and it must be annoying to listen to music and people shouting until the early hours every weekend in the summer, but David, he was incensed, like, proper demented, banging his cup on the side and kicking a filing cabinet." He paused at the sight of Smith's face. "What have I said?"

"He displayed violence."

"Yes."

"What else has he told you about the parties?"

Alan thought about it, searching his memory bank. "Well, that they ought to be shot for being so inconsiderate. That karma will visit them one day so they get their comeuppance." Realisation dawned, bright and sunny. "Is it him? Did he get arsey one time too many and kill them?"

"That's speculation on your part," Smith said, "but you know him better than we do. Would you say he was capable of what's been done? Have you read the latest about it? The methods of killing?"

Alan nodded.

"Can you see him doing that?" She leant forward, resting her forearms on the polished surface.

"Well, no, if I'm honest."

She sighed. Defeated?

He rushed on. "I can't see *anyone* doing it, but they do, don't they. Could he have just snapped?" Nauseated, Alan rubbed his chest. "Why would a party or two upset him to such a degree, though?"

"We all have bugbears," she said. "Maybe the noise level got too much. Maybe the constant parties throughout the summer wore the killer down. We have no motive at the moment, but this one could be plausible."

The man, Wilkins, appeared sceptical. Like he didn't think someone would lose their shit over a get-together. Smith, on the other hand . . . Now she was buying it. She'd stuffed it in her shopping basket and was racing for the till. Alan, well, he was on the fence. He tried to imagine David going off on one and killing his neighbours, but it didn't seem possible.

"Look, forget I said anything. I'm probably tired, entertaining things that don't exist." He pressed his fingertips to his gritty eyes then lowered his hands to lay them flat on the table. "I've basically accused him of murder. I feel bad."

"Don't. What you've said has been very interesting." Smith rose. "He's going to know it was you who called in, you realise that, don't you?"

Alan nodded. "I don't think he spoke to anyone else in the staffroom about mass killings. The other teachers would have said if he did. They'd have been shocked and gossiped about him, whereas I kept it to myself apart from talking to the head about the chat sessions."

Wilkins got up and walked to the door. "We'll see ourselves out."

Smith handed him a card. "If you think of anything else, please give me a ring. If something comes of this, you'll be needed in court if David pleads not guilty."

"What? You're going to arrest him?"

She smiled. "I hope so."

They left, and Alan slumped back, his mind going a mile a minute.

"Fucking hell's bells . . ."

CHAPTER TWENTY-FIVE

Bethany had ignored David for long enough. It was closing in on three a.m., and she wanted this first interview over and done with. Because he hadn't been arrested, she was sailing close to the wind here. He could complain about her for leaving him in a holding cell when he hadn't been formally charged. The warrant had been granted quickly — colour her shocked — and Isabelle and her second team were busy rooting through David's place. Bethany had hoped for news before going in for the chat, but life didn't always work out the way she wanted.

If he stuck to his ridiculous story regarding the rope and sabre, there wasn't much she could do about it until the items had been seized and tested by forensics. All right, the rope was probably common and found in many households, but if it and the sabre had DNA on them relating to the victims, David was well and truly in the shit.

She'd asked for him to be taken to an interview room — not the soft one, that would bring him a modicum of comfort, and she wanted him worried and on edge, likely to explode into that anger Alan Hughes had told them about. She'd prod him and see what happened.

With Mike by her side, she walked down the corridor and entered the room. She'd requested for Tammy to join them so she'd get a feel for how Bethany worked. Tammy needed to fit into the team, and learning all she could before doing her DC exams would help her immensely.

Tammy stood beside the door, and Bethany nodded at her in greeting. David sat on the other side of the table, no solicitor present. After all, they were just talking, he hadn't been charged with anything, so there was no need for one — unless he requested it or admitted to a crime.

Bethany and Mike sat opposite him.

"Can you take these cuffs off?" David stared down at his hands which rested on the table. "Someone took the others off when I was put in the cell, then they put these on when they got me out. They chafe."

"Not at present, no. You lunged at me in your home, remember, and I'm not about to put myself and my colleagues at risk." Bethany set the tape to record and said the usual to begin the interview. "Now, David, do you have something to tell us?"

"What about?"

"Oh, I don't know. Is there anything on your mind?"

"Only that I'm stuck in here and I'll be going into work having had no sleep."

Hopefully you won't be teaching those children again.

"Let's discuss your irritation about the parties in Le Huray Close," she said.

He blinked. Cogs working in his brain?

She pressed on. "We have it on good authority that you expressed anger to someone regarding them and mentioned the residents needed shooting. Explain that, please."

His cheeks coloured, and his lips drew up tight. "Be honest here. Could you stand living somewhere with that going on? We're talking starting the parties about six in the evening and continuing until the next day. A *whole night*. How would you feel about that?"

"I wouldn't be happy but would call the police and the environmental health department. That's the best way of dealing with things like that."

"I did call the police." His eyes narrowed, as though he recalled how he'd requested assistance and it hadn't been to his liking.

"Yes, we saw the logs over the years, although you refrained from ringing us for the last three. Why is that?"

"It was pointless. Nothing got done. You lot came out, then the parties continued as before. Sometimes even louder."

"So why not contact the council? They would have asked you to keep a diary and possibly record the noise level. Standard procedure."

"I realised it would be as useless as the police."

"But you didn't even try, so you've been suffering unnecessarily. It could all have been stopped years ago." She stared at him. Hard.

"Another neighbour called them. Again, nothing got done."

"What did you mean about shooting the residents? That ties in with your conversation about the mass school killings in America. Did you feel like doing the same to the people in Le Huray?"

"That was a throwaway comment."

"Right. How long have you been climbing?"

The change of subject seemed to throw him off, and his mouth hung open. "I . . . I've only just started."

"When did you purchase the rope?"

"Last week."

"Where?"

"Homebase."

"Do you have a receipt?"

"No."

"Cash or card?"

"Cash."

"We'll be checking CCTV. Where did you buy your sabre?"

"From a car boot sale."

Clever bastard. No trail. No proof he didn't. "When?"

"A month ago."

"Which car boot?"

"The one by Shadwell Hill. It's there every Sunday."

"Ah, that's handy. Did you practise climbing while you were in the area?"

"Of course not."

She leant back, affecting a calm demeanour. "What do you think about karaoke?"

He shuddered. "A hideous invention."

"When did you buy the microphone?"

His eyes widened slightly. "I don't know what you mean."

"You know, the microphone."

He shook his head.

Her phone rang. *For fuck's sake.* "Excuse me for a moment. DI Bethany Smith is leaving the room at three-twenty a.m." She paused the tape and left.

Isabelle's name was on the screen.

"Hi," Bethany said, leaning against the corridor wall.

"Receipt found."

Her stomach rolled over. "What for?"

"Food, purchased on Friday evening at five-fifty-seven, Sainsbury's."

"What is it?"

"Scotch eggs, cocktail sausages, bread, cheese, amongst other items."

"Brilliant. Anything else?"

"Not yet. Speak later."

"Okay, I just had to nip out of his interview, so message me next time." Bethany returned to the room and sat, then started the recording again. "DI Bethany Smith has returned to the room. Interview proceeding at three-twenty-three a.m." She sighed. "God, I could murder a picnic."

David scrunched his forehead. Mike coughed and hid his smile with a fist.

"I love a good cheese sandwich, don't you, David?" she asked. "Can't beat it, especially when you have a scotch egg and little sausages with it."

"What?" His cheeks gained a deeper hue.

"Do you like those things?" she asked.

"Um, yes?"

"Eat them recently, did you?"

"Not that I recall."

"So why did you buy them on Friday then?"

"I . . . Oh, yes. I did. I forgot, that's all."

"Enjoy them, did you?"

"Yes."

"Is your sabre blunt?"

"Pardon?"

"Is it blunt? You know, so you don't cut anyone or anything when you're fencing."

"I don't know what you're getting at."

"I stated it simply enough but will repeat it. I get that you must be tired. Is. Your. Sabre. Blunt?"

He shook his head.

"Mr Chesterfield has shaken his head." She raised her eyebrows. "Does that gesture mean no, it's not blunt, or that you're exasperated by my question?"

He clamped his mouth shut.

The air seemed to thicken, and she wondered if he'd noticed it, too. Was it affecting him? Sending him closer to the edge? "Where do you go fencing?"

"I . . ."

"It's just that the closest place to do that is in the city, and we're a good fifteen to twenty minutes away from there. Do you go to Fantastic Fencing, David? Or is it something you do by yourself? I've heard YouTube is amazing for learning things."

"Yes, I teach myself from YouTube."

She reckoned he'd grasped that as a lifeline. He'd played right into her hands. Top bloke. "So your home laptop and any you use at school, plus your phone, perhaps, will reflect you watching tutorial videos?"

"You can't touch them without a warrant."

"Oh, we have one. Officers have been in your house for quite some time."

He remained silent, but his hands shook.

I'm getting to him.

"Then again, you're an IT/computing teacher, so you'd know how to erase certain searches, wouldn't you. The thing is, as you probably know, that means nothing to digital forensics. They can find *everything* on devices. You should read up on it sometime. Fascinating how fast they can draw out data."

"This conversation seems pointless," he blustered, straightening his shoulders. "I would like to go home now."

"I'm sure you would. Same here, but I'm afraid we have a bit more to discuss before we can hit the hay. Do you like toast?"

"Look, this is utter bollocks."

"Please answer the question."

"Yes, I like toast."

"What about filing cabinets?"

"Excuse me?"

"Do they make you angry, David?"

"Of course not!"

"So why kick one then?"

He appeared truly perplexed. "I don't get what you're on about."

"You kicked one in anger when talking about how the parties made you feel."

"I want a solicitor."

"Why do you need one?"

"To stop this farce."

"That's fine. We'll appoint one of your choice or call the duty in. Which would you prefer?"

"Anyone. Just get them in here."

"That may take some time, I'm afraid. We'd have to call them, get them out of bed. We'll pop you back in the holding cell in the meantime."

"Why can't I stay in here?"

"As I've expressed to you before, I fear for mine and my colleagues' safety where you're concerned, so a holding cell is the best place for you."

Her phone vibrated with a message. She pulled it out beneath the table and read it.

Isabelle: BLACK CLOTHING BUNDLED UP INSIDE A CARRIER BAG AND STUFFED BEHIND SOME BOXES IN THE BOTTOM OF A BUILT-IN WARDROBE. PAIR OF BOOTS WITH THE SAME TREAD AS THE MARKS ON KEITH'S FACE. I'VE RUN THE LIGHT OVER THEM. BLOOD.

Bethany: THANK YOU!

She stared at David. "Why is there dirty clothing and boots in a bag in your wardrobe? Don't you have a wash bin?" She smiled at him.

His face went arctic white. "I forgot to wash them."

"That was a bit remiss of you." Pause. Stare. Inhale. Exhale. "Why is there blood on them?"

He closed his eyes momentarily, then opened them and glared at her. "There isn't."

"Funny, our lead forensic officer says there is, and she knows her stuff. Will that blood be yours, Amanda DeBord's or Keith Trannor's?"

"Fuck off!" he roared and lurched across the table at her, looping his bound wrists around her neck and hauling her to him.

The edge of the table dug painfully into her thighs. She lifted her hands between his arms and chopped outwards, dipping, flattening her front to the table, extricating herself swiftly. By the time she stood upright, Mike and Tammy had whipped round and held David by his upper arms.

"I could arrest you for that," Bethany said, smoothing down her hair at the front where it had brushed against his chest. "David Chesterfield just assaulted DI Bethany Smith." Assault was a bit strong, but it sounded better. She gave him a filthy look. "Sit." She pointed at his chair. "Answer my question."

Mike and Tammy manhandled him onto his seat. David struggled, trying to shrug them off, face screwed up, his gaze on her. They maintained their grip on him.

"I'm not answering anything else until my solicitor gets here," David snarled.

"Fine. I'll sort that now for you." She took her phone out and rang Ursula, requesting the duty, then slid it back in her pocket. Sat. Smiled again. "I've changed my mind about the holding cell. We'll just take a breather here until your brief arrives. I'll keep the tape running because you've shown you can get angry and fly off the handle. I wouldn't want to put us in a position where you did something to one of us and it wasn't on tape. Mind you, there's the camera up there in the corner, so that'll capture everything."

He turned his head and gazed that way. "Whoever is watching this, listen to me carefully. I want you to know I'm going to make a complaint. The treatment I've suffered is disgusting. I've done nothing wrong." He faced Bethany again, 'smug' written in self-righteous ink on his forehead.

"Nothing wrong in your eyes but very wrong in the eyes of the law?" She folded her arms over her chest. "Let's play word association while we wait."

He sighed.

"Aww, come on, it'll be fun, I promise you," she said. "I'll start." A heartbeat or two. "Copse."

No answer.

"Okay, I'll play by myself." She leant back. "Tree. Trunk. Body. Dead. Strangulation. Rope. Murder. Witness."

He sat upright at the last one.

"See. Watch. Observe."

He raised his hands to cover his face, fingertips disappearing beneath his fringe.

"Notice. Sign. Statement."

"No," he said, still hiding behind his palms.

"Evidence. Arrest. Conviction. Court. Prison."

"No!" He slammed his hands on the table and hung his head. "I couldn't stand it anymore. Couldn't stand *them.* They were inconsiderate. Laughed at me. Didn't care."

At last! "What was your objective?"

"To stop it. Noise. It got on my nerves. Too much. Maddening. I had to give my neighbours a break."

"Is that blood going to be Amanda's and Keith's? Are we going to find traces on your sabre?"

"Bleach. I scrubbed it."

"Doesn't matter."

"You can't . . . It wasn't meant to be this way."

"Did you kill all those people in Le Huray Close, David?" Her heart banged violently.

"Oh God, yes . . ."

"David Chesterfield, I am arresting you for the murders of Amanda DeBord, Dee Groocock, Jim Ody, Craig Gillan, Lisa Hicks, and Keith Trannor. You do not have to say anything, but it may harm your defence if you do not mention when questioned something which you later rely on in court. Anything you do say may be given in evidence. This interview is concluded at three-thirty-one a.m. until Mr Chesterfield's solicitor arrives."

She signed off and glanced at Mike. He grinned then tugged David upright with Tammy's help. Bethany opened the door, adrenaline speeding through her veins, her legs going to jelly. She followed Mike, Tammy and David into the corridor, already anticipating the next interview where she'd do her best to get all the details out of him, push him to reveal exactly what he'd done to those poor people.

While Mike and Tammy took David to a cell, Bethany pressed her back to the wall beside the front desk and closed her eyes. Vinny would have been proud of her for using the word association game. They'd played it in bed on the nights they hadn't been able to sleep, a surefire way to send them off. She hadn't thought David would crack, and when he had, she'd been surprised.

She opened her eyes to find Mike standing in front of her. He pulled her in for a hug, patting her back, and Tammy stood in the background, smiling.

"Think you can handle working with us?" Bethany asked her, easing out of Mike's hold and cocking her head at the young uniform.

"I'm going to love it," Tammy said.

"Well then, you can start straight away. Phone the remaining Le Huray residents. Find the number for a Vicky Trannor and give her a ring, too. Tell them all they're safe now. Yes, it's early hours, but it'll give you a chance to deal with people who might bite your head off for disturbing them. Practise your public relations voice. Then go home, because that's where I'm going."

She walked out and got in her car. Mike flopped into the passenger seat and belted up. They looked at each other in the darkness, Bethany resting the side of her head on the seat.

"Bloody word association?" he said.

"Yep, good, wasn't it?" She faced ahead and started the engine. "We have my husband to thank for that. He loved playing it. The idea just popped in my head."

"Good old Vinny." Mike chuckled. "I fucking miss him."

The familiar prickle of tears attacked her eyes. "Me, too, matey. More than you'll ever know."

She drove out of the car park, heading for Mike's. Maybe she'd crash at *his* place for a change. All this talk of Vinny had her not wanting to be alone at home. A lock of her hair brushed against her cheek, tickling, and she raised a hand to swipe it away, but there was nothing there. Vinny's laughter rang out in her head, and she smiled.

"You little sod," she said.

"What have I done?" Mike asked.

"Nothing. Just talking to myself."

"You'll be carted off to the loony bin if you keep that up."

She laughed along with her husband, her heart lighter than it had been for ages.

Life, despite her living it without Vinny, was good.

Bring on the next case.

THE END

THE JOFFE BOOKS STORY

We began in 2014 when Jasper agreed to publish his mum's much-rejected romance novel and it became a bestseller.

Since then we've grown into the largest independent publisher in the UK. We're extremely proud to publish some of the very best writers in the world, including Joy Ellis, Faith Martin, Caro Ramsay, Helen Forrester, Simon Brett and Robert Goddard. Everyone at Joffe Books loves reading and we never forget that it all begins with the magic of an author telling a story.

We are proud to publish talented first-time authors, as well as established writers whose books we love introducing to a new generation of readers.

We have been shortlisted for Independent Publisher of the Year at the British Book Awards three times, in 2020, 2021 and 2022, and for the Diversity and Inclusivity Award at the Independent Publishing Awards in 2022.

We built this company with your help, and we love to hear from you, so please email us about absolutely anything bookish at: feedback@joffebooks.com.

If you want to receive free books every Friday and hear about all our new releases, join our mailing list: www.joffebooks.com/contact

And when you tell your friends about us, just remember: it's pronounced Joffe as in coffee or toffee!

ALSO BY EMMY ELLIS

DI BETHANY SMITH
Book 1: THE COLD CALL KILLER
Book 2: THE CREEPY-CRAWLY KILLER
Book 3: THE SCREWDRIVER KILLER
Book 4: THE SCORCHED SKIN KILLER
Book 5: THE STREET PARTY KILLER

DETECTIVE CAROL WREN MYSTERIES
Book 1: SPITE YOUR FACE
Book 2: HOLD YOUR BREATH
Book 3: GUILT BURNS HOLES
Book 4: BEST SERVED COLD
Book 5: BLOOD RUNS DEEP

Printed in Great Britain
by Amazon

60207603R00119